## WILL THE REAL MAGGIE HOWELL SHINE THROUGH!

Whatever he had to say must have been really hard for him, and I wanted to help him. I wanted to say, "I love you too, Rob. It's okay. I know we're young, but say it. We'll work it out." But before I could open my mouth, he blurted out, "All that makeup is wrong for you, Maggie. It makes you look funny. And I kinda like your freckles."

Then he hurried off before I could say anything—something nasty or clever to cover my hurt feelings. He had totally caught me by surprise. All this time I thought he was having a hard time asking me for a date. And all he had stopped me for was to tell me I looked funny.

But he did say he liked my freckles. . . .

# FIFTEEN #

## BARBARA STEINER

# IS THERE A CURE FOR SOPHOMORE YEAR?

A SIGNET VISTA BOOK

NEW AMERICAN LIBRARY

## PUBLISHER'S NOTE

This novel is a work of fiction. Names, characters, places, and incidents either are the product of the author's imagination or are used fictitiously, and any resemblance to actual persons, living or dead, events, or locales is entirely coincidental.

NAL BOOKS ARE AVAILABLE AT QUANTITY DISCOUNTS WHEN USED TO PROMOTE PRODUCTS OR SERVICES. FOR INFORMATION PLEASE WRITE TO PREMIUM MARKETING DIVISION, NEW AMERICAN LIBRARY, 1633 BROADWAY, NEW YORK, NEW YORK 10019.

RL 4.5/IL 5+

SIGNET VISTA TRADEMARK REG. U.S. PAT. OFF. AND FOREIGN COUNTRIES
REGISTERED TRADEMARK—MARCA REGISTRADA
HECHO EN CHICAGO, U.S.A.

SIGNET, SIGNET CLASSIC, MENTOR, PLUME, MERIDIAN and NAL BOOKS are published by New American Library, 1633 Broadway, New York, New York 10019

First Printing, January, 1986

3   4   5   6   7   8   9

PRINTED IN THE UNITED STATES OF AMERICA

# *Chapter 1*

"Look at these, Maggie." Carol dangled a pair of earrings in front of my nose. "They're perfect. Hold them up to your ears."

I sighed longingly. No matter how many times I tried to explain my parents to Carol, she'd never truly understand my situation. It was only too clear to me, however. I was the victim of a conspiracy between two adults, both of whom were bound and determined not to let me, their only child, grow up—ever. How could I explain that to Carol, especially when her parents rank among the rich and beautiful people of Cedarhurst? Although I'd never been at Carol's at the hour of seven-thirty A.M., I was absolutely certain she didn't face the kind of regimental inspection I went through every morning before I left for school.

I looked at the green bead and silver leaf combination. Behind the display was a mirror and I swept back my hair and held them up to my earlobes. Gorgeous and sophisticated, they'd hang at least two inches past my ear. I could just feel them swaying seductively. I had let my hair get long and tiny earrings were totally hidden unless I pulled it back into a ponytail.

"That green is one of your colors, Maggie,"

Carol said. "I can't believe you don't wash in all those red highlights."

"The same sun that gives me red streaks gives me the freckles, Carol," I said. "It's a trade-off."

Carol's hair was blond and styled with a short cut, wedged in the back. She was wearing long earrings but looked equally cute with small ones since they showed up well.

Debra Dennison wore super long earrings and her ear cuff had a dangle on it too. Debra can pull that off, though. She's a dancer and her hair is thick and exotic looking—well, her hair isn't exotic, just the styles she does it in. A bun with tendrils escaping or woven-together braids, topknots. She's super good with arranging it.

Carol had taken the earrings from me and her green eyes sparkled as she waved them back and forth, tempting me, but I knew better. I picked them out of her hand and hooked the plastic display card back over a row on the revolving tree.

Carol looked surprised, and Debra, my oldest best friend, tried to help me explain. "You don't have any idea how hard we worked to get Maggie's mom to even let her get her ears pierced, Carol," Debra said.

"Yeah, and then I got permission only because Mom once went shopping for a new pair of clip-on earrings for herself and found they went out of style in 1954. When she finally decided she had to get her own ears pierced, she couldn't very well keep saying no to me. So we went and did it together. I literally had to hold her hand," I said with a laugh.

Debra smiled. "Then when you went home your dad nearly killed both of you."

All three of us laughed at that, but I couldn't help thinking that if Carol and Deb had to *live* with parents as backward as mine, they'd stop laughing and start squirming.

Well, at first all I did was squirm. That was three years ago. At twelve you can handle Stone Age rules and regulations a little bit easier. All I wanted to do at that age was get a bra, but finally even I had to admit that I'd be spending a lot of money for nothing. Instead I settled for an extra-large sweat shirt that said SAVE THE SEALS and three Bonne Belle lip smackers. I can still fit into the sweat shirt and I have one lip ice left. Root Beer. No one but my dog liked the taste; and being kissed by a two-ton Old English Sheep dog has never been one of my intimate fantasies.

At thirteen I did start to protest, however, and toyed with the idea of ordering one of those custom T-shirts that said THESE PARENTS UNFAIR TO TEENS. By October I even threatened to stop eating, but Mom knew from past experience that I would never be a candidate for anorexia. Sometimes I can even eat Dad under the table, and since I'm blessed with the metabolism of a hummingbird, it never shows. In the end, nothing worked; so now the same old rules, plus a few new ones, have been ratified and passed despite my attempt at veto.

At that moment, Carol elbowed me in the ribs. There I was, daydreaming again. She reminded me that I wasn't home, but out on probation for only a few minutes longer. "Look, there's Rob Tyler. Bet he'd notice you if you were wearing these." She picked up the earrings again. "You could put them on after you left home."

All three of us moved to the rack near the door. Sure enough, Rob Tyler, Jamie Patterson, and Dobs Cartwright were sauntering through the mall in their tight jeans. The guys held giant cups of Boardwalk fries and were greedily shoving them into their mouths. Jamie's back pocket bulged with a can of Copenhagen, but I bet it was for show. What girl would want to kiss a guy who chewed tobacco?

Thinking of kissing twice in that many minutes started another scene spinning in my head: I was dressed in a white toga trimmed with silver braid. Long, sparkling chains dangled from my ears as I held a bunch of grapes over Rob Tyler's waiting lips. "Your kisses are sweeter than any grapes," he whispered.

"Forbidden fruit," I whispered back, teasing him so that he totally lost control of himself and swept me into his arms.

"What are you mooning about now, Maggie Howell? Come clean." Debra shook me out of my daydream. "You have a very wicked gleam in your eye."

"There are some thoughts that a woman prefers to keep to herself," I said, then grinned, trying my best to look knowing.

"I'll bet. For someone with your imagination, Maggie, you sure don't have much nerve." Carol decided to buy the two pairs of earrings she'd picked out along with the pair I wished I could have had. "As tall as you are, you need some really dramatic earrings. Not those dumb little things you have to hunt through a curtain of hair to find."

"Look, I know that. You know it. Just convince my mom." Resigned to my fate, cursing whatever ancestors had willed Mom her conservative genes, I left the store empty-handed.

"You're the only one who isn't allowed to wear dangling earrings. It's no big deal," Carol continued. "Why doesn't your mom worry about your hanging out with the wrong crowd or flunking algebra or something really serious?"

"She does that too, Carol. Believe Maggie," Debra broke in. "Mrs. Howell is a wonderful person, but in some areas she's as unflexible as the Rock of Gibraltar."

I added my final argument. "Look, Carol, spending the next three years totally grounded is my miserable fate if I break the rules."

"Okay, enough about your parents, Maggie," said Debra. "How would you like to spend the next fifteen minutes? You said you had to be home at five-thirty."

So I did, and Debra had been friends with me long enough to know Mom would probably call in a missing-persons report at exactly 5:45.

"I guess I have enough money for an Orange Julius." I pulled out the change from the bottom of my purse and started to count.

"I'm buying." Carol whipped out a twenty-dollar bill without even having to rummage through her bag.

"Is that this week's allowance, or left over from last week?" Debra remarked with a hint of sarcasm. I noticed it, but either Carol didn't care or she chose to ignore Debra's tone—which I thought was neat. I'll say this for Carol. She may be spoiled, as my Mom says, but she's also generous. In her cattier moments Debra says Carol is showing off, but I happen to know that Carol just never thinks about money.

I find that almost impossible to imagine. My dad thought that five dollars a week was too much allowance until I pointed out that it was the price of one movie. Unless you go to a matinee. But of course no one goes to the movies in the afternoon unless it's the third rainy Sunday in a row, and you're burned out on Trivial Pursuit.

"Thanks, Carol. But I'd better run." Debra smiled at us both. While she sometimes gave Carol a hard time, I knew that, deep down, she liked Carol as much as I did. After all, Carol couldn't help it if her parents were millionaires.

"I thought you didn't have a class today," I called after her.

"I don't, but I told Mom I'd help her close up early. She has a date." Debra waved and then headed for the east door of the mall. We waved back and turned to the counter to order the frothy orange drinks that were our favorites. Mindy Patton, a junior in our school, was working behind the counter. She stirred up extra-large cups for us, much to my delight.

I wouldn't mind having an afterschool job like Mindy's but unfortunately I wasn't old enough to work. Honestly, sometimes I think being fifteen has to be one of life's worst practical jokes. You're too old for things like jacks and dolls and junior-league ball, and too young for just about everything else. I've never been good at softball anyway; even though a sports career was my dad's fantasy. Although I'm not good enough to go out for the team sports at school, I think I just might be a fantastic actress. But then sophomores never get parts in plays at Hammond High. We're considered too young, too inexperienced. Worst of all, I'm too young to go out on a date (my mom says) or get a job unless my parents sign working papers. They won't. Dad says I'll have to work soon enough; in the meantime I can baby-sit if I need extra cash. So what *can* I do? Hang out at the mall and drown my sorrows in orange juice.

Rules, rules, rules. And who makes them up? Parents. Schools. Teachers.

"Do you ever feel like the world is just one big prison, Carol?"

"Huh? Oh yeah, sure." Carol had finished her drink and was bending her straw into weird shapes. She tried to be sympathetic, I knew. But her life was so different from mine. Her parents were easy on her. How could she really understand?

One thing neither of us could imagine, though, was the idea of our moms dating, as Debra's did. We'd both talked about that before.

"Do you think Debra likes teaching those dance classes, Maggie? Or does she do it because they need the money?" I was surprised at her question; maybe Carol was more perceptive than I had thought.

"Some of both, I guess." Debra had been helping her mom at the dance studio for a couple of years, and I knew that this year she was teaching three beginning classes herself. I never questioned whether or not she enjoyed it. I just knew she was good at it, so I figured she liked it okay. Then again, she probably didn't have a choice. Her mom and dad had gotten divorced years ago, and her mom had started the dance studio just to survive.

No, I didn't envy Debra's life the way I did Carol's. Debra worked because she had to, and she didn't have much time for fun. Also, even though my dad was tough on me, I was used to having him around. I didn't want to change things *that* much. Of course, if Mom worked someplace other than at home, she wouldn't always be around. Maybe then she wouldn't hover over me so much.

We had to run for the bus, but got home on time. "Hi, kids," Mom said as we walked in and tossed our books on the coffee table. I gritted my teeth, a habit my dentist says I'll regret some day. When was Mom going to stop calling us *kids*?

"Hi, Mom. What's for supper? Hi, Gerard. Have you been a good dog?" Gerard barked his answer so loudly I could hardly hear my mother's reply.

"Pot roast—it's in the crock pot. Your dad called. He'll be half an hour late, so I said we'd wait. That means I'll have time to type five more pages."

Suddenly I had this funny thought. Did Dad always have to check in and say he'd be late or tell Mom where he was like I did? Maybe Mom was the whole problem, and it wasn't a conspiracy as I'd been assuming.

"Could you and Carol make a salad? Everything is in the crisper," she called out from her office.

Our house has three bedrooms and a basement. We've divided the space up so that Dad has the basement for his saw and junk, and Mom took the extra bedroom for her office. She types and edits, mostly for three romance writers in town. Sometimes she says she's about ready to write one herself. She thinks she has the formula memorized by now.

Carol and I talked about her books as we took out the salad fixings. Soon we started to giggle. "He crushed her willing body into his," Carol whispered.

"Her heart pounded and liquid fire flowed to her very toes, leaving her powerless to object."

"Yeah, Dobs Cartwright would find me powerless to object," Carol said in a low voice as she began peeling carrots. Suddenly, she grabbed up a bunch of the thin, orange curls and plopped them on top of my head. "Her orange curls framed her face as she gazed into his dark eyes."

" 'You look good enough to nibble,' he said as his nose twitched and his whiskers vibrated." I squealed and flipped the carrot peels off my head into the sink. One landed on Carol's shirt.

" '*Mon petit chou*,' he murmured." Carol couldn't stop. "That means, my little cabbage." Within

minutes we were laughing so hard we were totally incapacitated.

"What's so funny about a salad?" Mom asked
suspiciously as she returned to the kitchen to
peer into the crock pot and dish out the roast
and potatoes.

I quickly began shredding the lettuce as I
wiped the tears from my eyes. Mom came over
and hugged us, one in each arm. "You two. Ah,
to be fifteen again."

That sobered me up enough to get out the
ranch-style dressing and pour it into a prettier
dish.

Soon Dad came in, and a little while later we
sat down to dinner in the alcove off the kitchen.
Although we have a formal dining room, we
only use it about twice a year and on holidays.

"You spending the night, Carol?" Dad asked,
reaching for seconds on roast.

"Yes, sir." Carol put on her formal just-for-
parents voice. Naturally, my parents loved it.
"My mother and father have a rally in Denver."

"Think your dad will be elected DA again?"

"Oh, I suppose so. I don't pay much attention."

"You will when he runs for governor someday."

"Maybe. I'll be on my own by then, though."

Carol was on her own *now* as far as I could
see. She had her own money, and she was going
to get a car when she turned sixteen. And with a
housekeeper and a cook at her house, there
weren't even any chores for her to do. Her
parents trusted her, treated her like an adult.
She was lucky.

"Thank you for a delicious dinner, Mrs. Howell," Carol said as we finished. I stood up to clear our dishes.

"Let's all wash dishes and then go to the movies," Dad suggested, looking at his watch. "If we catch the seven-thirty show we won't be out too late."

"There's no school tomorrow," I reminded him. "Quarter break."

"Oh, Dave, I can't," Mom protested. "I promised Marty I'd have her manuscript finished by Monday morning. Her publisher is calling her every day now. Besides, everything they're showing is rated R. I don't understand why they can't make more family films."

I couldn't understand why Mom wouldn't let me see an R movie. Carol and Debra saw them all the time. I always feel foolish when everyone at school is talking about the latest flick, and I have to admit I'm not allowed to go see it.

"There's not even anything on TV worth watching," Mom continued. "It's all soaps, now, every night." I remembered with a thrill that "Destinies," my favorite soap, was on. Carol liked that show as much as I did, but we'd have to be careful about watching it. Mom practically monitored my TV viewing as closely as she did my movie choices.

"How are you ever going to get to know anything about real life?" Carol whispered as we put away the rest of the dishes that Dad had washed. (The dishwasher was on the fritz again.)

"You'll have to tell me," I whispered back. "Let's go upstairs before Dad wants to play Triv-

ial Pursuit." My life was trivial enough as it was,
I thought disgustedly. "As soon as Mom gets
busy typing again, we can sneak back down and
turn on 'Destinies.' "

"Great," Carol said.

"Then afterward, we can make some popcorn
and listen to the new Springsteen record you
got. At least Mom hasn't caught on to how decadent today's music is."

"Careful. She probably has a waltz collection.
Surely we'd like to hear them. . . ." Carol was
catching on at last. I didn't know why she liked
to come to my house, but I was glad she did.
Much as I loved Debra, meeting Carol was the
best thing that had happened to me this fall.

"Oh, I forgot. Mom says I can have a pool
party tomorrow night because of quarter break,"
she said as we climbed up the stairs to my room.

"You forgot! Carol, how could you?"

"Actually I was saving it for a surprise. Want
to hear who I've invited?"

"Do I?" Gerard took my eager tone of voice
as an invitation to join me on the bed as I sat
down. I think Dad had surreptitiously fed him
some of the smelly cheese he likes to eat for
dessert, because Gerard had the worse case of
bad breath. I screamed, then nearly choked with
laughter as Carol said, "His curly white hair hid
his brooding eyes from me, but I knew that
finally I had captured his attention."

# *Chapter 2*

We slept late and then I suspect Mom finally sent Gerard upstairs to get us up. He leaped onto the bed and started licking my face.

"Yuck, Gerard, get off." I hated to be awakened abruptly.

Carol was one of those awful people who can wake up immediately, and when the covers next to me began to shake, I knew she was laughing. "Some alarm clock." She sat up, stretched, and then hopped out of bed. "I thought it was my little brother Sam. I'm hungry. Come on. Then after breakfast I have to get home and supervise the party food. If I leave it up to Nadia, she'll do something fancy, and I want real-people food."

Entering the kitchen in our bathrobes, we found homemade sweet rolls on the table, along with a tub of whipped butter, orange juice, and glasses all set out. A note with a smile face said, "Enjoy." But Mom stopped typing when she heard us.

" 'Morning, girls. Sleep well?"

"Yes, Mrs. Howell." Carol was being extra polite, and I suspected what was coming next. "I'm having a small pool party tonight for some of my new friends—to celebrate surviving a quarter of the school year. May Maggie come? My parents, as well as the rest of our staff, will be home."

Mom looked at me. How could she refuse such a masterful invitation? "I guess so, Carol. Sounds like fun."

"Someone will bring her home," Carol continued, "but it might be after ten since we'll have to help clean up afterward."

"I guess we can stretch the curfew since it's Friday night."

I wished Carol would ask me to spend the night sometime. I couldn't help being curious about why she didn't, but I had decided not to question her. I was just glad Mom didn't do anything to mess up our plans for the party.

After we ate, Carol called home and arranged for someone to come get her. "Which suit are you going to wear tonight, Maggie? Let me see it before Charles gets here," Carol asked as she was making the bed she had slept in.

"Which suit? You've got to be kidding." I rummaged through a dresser drawer and pulled out the Speedo tank suit I'd worn all summer. Then I tugged it on while Carol finished getting dressed. The scream I let out made her drop her curling iron. She turned to look at me and covered her mouth, trying not to laugh.

"Oh, Maggie, you look like a Jimmy Dean sausage, just bursting with flavor."

"I've gained weight this fall. I knew my jeans were getting a little tight, but—"

"It's not weight, Maggie, but some curves at last. Not that you're exactly voluptuous yet, but

. . ." She giggled again. I felt embarrassed and pleased at the same time.

"What are you going to do? You can't wear that tonight." We heard a horn honk, and Carol looked outside the window. "Oh, here's my ride. Good luck. I know you'll think of something."

For a few minutes, I just stood there in front of the mirror, staring. Then, "Mom!" I screamed after Carol had gone and ran down the stairs. "Look. It's awful."

Mom looked up from her typewriter. "I see what you mean, honey. But I wouldn't call it *awful.*"

"I would. I can't wear this thing tonight. I'd rather die."

"No, you're right. You can't. It looks vulgar." Then she caught my expression. "I don't mean your body is vulgar, Maggie. It's just the way the suit fits." She got up from her chair and came over and gave me a big hug. "My baby is growing up."

I squirmed loose. "What can I do, Mom? Can we . . . could you . . ."

She sighed. "Yes, I guess so. Go get dressed and we'll zip down to the mall. Bathing suits should be on sale, if anyone has any left." She looked down at her typewriter. "I guess I can work late again tonight."

"Thanks, Mom. I just can't wear this body stocking tonight, and the party won't be any fun unless I can go swimming with everybody else."

Visions of sexy bikinis danced in my head as I pulled on jeans and a sweat shirt. As I struggled with the zipper, I realized that the jeans *were* tighter than they used to be. I just had to look nice tonight since Carol said she'd invited Rob Tyler, Dobs Cartwright, and Jamie Patterson. She didn't know if they'd come, of course, but at least they hadn't said no. I got butterflies in my stomach just thinking about the evening. As juniors and varsity football players, they were dead center in Hammond High's circle of popular people.

Mom had thrown on her Levi's and a checked flannel shirt. She'd been working in her bathrobe. Some days I'd seen her type till noon in that plaid flannel bathrobe. She glanced in the car mirror. "My hair's dirty, but I guess it won't matter. With any luck, we'll just sneak in and back out, lickety-split."

The Denver Dry Goods had a few bathing suits left, but they were all too large. I hadn't grown or filled out *that* much. It was the same story at Fashion Bar.

"Oh, dear, this is going to take all day, Maggie. How about a tank suit? The sporting goods—"

"Mom. I can't wear a tank suit now." I shuddered at the idea of getting out of the pool all wet and having a suit mold itself to my body. Tank suits were either for girls with great figures or for competitors who didn't care about anything but medals.

"Okay, we'll try May D&F, but let's move the car." We drove to the opposite end of the mall and hit the other big department stores there. We had better luck. There were three suits that were definite possibilities. I had tried each one on twice and was surprised to find the almost-bikini didn't look too bad because you could get the top and bottom pieces in different sizes if you wanted to.

"Mom?" I took two steps out into the hall of the dressing room.

"I like the green one. It looks marvelous with your hair and brown eyes." Her voice was firm, her decision made.

Taking one last look at the pink bikini, I decided I'd better not press my luck. Mom had brought me to town. She was willing to pay the higher price for the green suit, which even on sale wasn't cheap. And at least it was two-piece. I put it back on. The top was a little loose, but the next size smaller looked too tight. How typical for me that I would be in between sizes.

I handed it over the door to her, and she went to pay while I pulled on my jeans and shirt.

We headed home. Mom went back to work, and I went upstairs to try on my suit three more times. By evening, I was horribly nervous and found myself almost wishing that Carol had invited only girls to her party.

Dad drove me over to the Barton's place. "Now this is what I call the good life!" he said, glancing around at the huge house and grounds. "But I sure am glad I don't have to mow this lawn."

"You wouldn't have to if you lived here, Dad. They have lots of help."

He grinned. "Have fun, Maggie. Hope you'll be able to stand coming home to Poverty Row."

I laughed and jumped out of the car. I estimated that the Bartons had about four acres. Their house was in an area called Lake Shore Estates. IBM executives, lawyers, doctors, and other privileged Cedarhurst families lived here. The properties surrounded a small man-made lake so you could have a sailboat or wind surfer. Carol had told me that they owned two canoes too. I had seen the place by day when we'd dropped Carol off, but until now she had never invited us over.

Debra and I had met Carol the first day of high school when we saw her wandering around looking lost and even newer than we looked. Debra and I had come from the same junior high, Pueblo, into Hammond; Carol came from Travis. It usually feeds into Fairview, but Carol said her parents had decided Hammond had as good college-prep courses as even the private schools did, and there was someone available to drive her the extra distance until she had her own car.

Carol's best friend had moved away during the summer, so she was grateful to us for befriending her that first day. After that, we'd hit it off so well we became a trio. Sometimes three friends can't get along as well as two, but maybe because we were each so different, we made it work. Debra has a lot of self-confidence, and I, I have to admit, am the most mature. Carol is more sophisticated and experienced about a lot of things. And while that may make me sound like the dud of the group, I have some great ideas to contribute. But I need Carol's nerve to help me carry them out.

I spotted Deb coming toward the house from a different direction. "Debra, hi. We could have picked you up."

"That's okay. Mom and her friend Carl were going to a movie. They dropped me off on their way."

"Aren't you excited?" I asked as we began walking up the path. "Carol has kept her place so secret from us. I'm dying to see it. Not to mention who might be here."

"Do you think the guys will come?"

"Part of me hopes they will. Part of me hopes they won't. Isn't that funny?"

"No, I feel the same way. I guess I'm stuck with Jamie, though, since you and Carol have dibs on the other two. Or what if Rob falls for me instead of you?"

"I'll drown you. Beware!"

"Just try." We both started to run toward the house.

"Wow, look at this." We'd gone directly to the pool area. It was so funny to think I'd never been to Carol's house since she'd practically lived at my place the last month. Behind the pool was a house almost the size of mine. I imagined that it had bathrooms and places to change, probably showers.

"My Lord!" The food was awesome. "Hold me back. I didn't eat dinner." Debra went closer. There were a whole bunch of tables covered with real cloths, red checkered, and there was a pile of napkins to match. The charcoal grill was fired up, and next to it sat mounds of hot dogs, hamburgers, buns, potato salad, chips, dips, baked beans, two cakes, fruit . . . and at the end of the table a man was filling an ice cream freezer with ice and salt.

"Maggie. Deb. Think this will be enough food?"

"For how long, Carol? Are we staying all weekend?"

Carol laughed. "Mom says you can never have too much food at a party where there'll be teenage boys."

"I don't see the boys. Do you see any boys, Maggie?" Debra pretended to look around.

"Wait and see." Carol smiled. "I invited some backups if the terrific trio doesn't come." Other kids began arriving; and after helping ourselves to Cokes, Debra and I changed into our suits in the pool house. Even though so far everyone had admired my new suit, I kept on my sweat shirt till we were ready to swim. The air got cool as soon as the sun went down, but the pool was heated. There was an outdoor fireplace for heat and roasting hot dogs if you wanted to do your own. What an incredible setup. I could hardly believe it. Lucky Carol. Who wouldn't want to come to a party here? I couldn't picture throwing a party at my house even if Mom would let me have one.

The evening was in full swing when Rob, Jamie, and Dobs sauntered in. Carol was hostess, so she had to get out of the pool and show them where to dress. I stayed in the deep water, submerged up to my chin, treading water.

Debra swam over to me. "Now what do we do?"

"You could always swim up to Jamie and say, 'Hi, there. I'm Debra. I like you.' You know— the direct approach."

"Could you do that?"

"No. But you're much more outgoing than I am, and good at communicating. Maybe I'll pretend I'm drowning just as they get in the water."

Debra laughed. "Harold Tubbs would come to your rescue."

"Yeah, with my luck that's exactly what would happen." At first I wondered why Carol had invited Harold, but then I figured out what must have happened. She'd invited a lot of people in her classes, and gradually the word got around that there was a party. That's the way it works in Cedarhurst. It's pretty casual, and people don't always worry about being invited. There were only a few juniors at the party, though, and frankly I was surprised that the football trio had showed up.

I watched from a dark corner of the pool as they joined the laughing, splashing crowd. They swam a few laps, then paused at the side, talking to each other, not mingling at all.

I felt a foot on my head and jerked away before anyone could push me under.

"Maggie, get out. You're going to get all shriveled up." It was Carol. She looked so good in her bright yellow bikini that I felt like crying.

Quickly I climbed up the ladder at the deep end and grabbed my beach towel. "Brrrr. It's cold."

"It is *not* that cold. Let me see how your suit looks when it's wet."

I opened the towel to give her a quick peek. Then I twisted my hands around the ends and drew it closer around my body.

"Cute. Dry off and then act natural. Guys aren't attracted to terry-covered mummies."

"Some may be. Do you think you know everything?"

"I told you they'd come, didn't I? Want another Coke?"

"Not yet." My teeth had started to chatter, which wasn't very attractive either. How could Carol walk around as if it was midsummer? I never realized it'd be so cold at night. I moved in closer to the fire.

"Hi, Maggie." Harold Tubbs had found me. Ugh. I'd had the great good fortune to go all the way through grade school and junior high with Harold. He wasn't *too* bad, just overweight, his teeth still in braces, and he was always in need of a haircut. Even when styles were longer, Harold's hair never seemed to look right. It had a style all its own. "You cold?" he asked.

"Yeah, a little. How can you tell?" I asked, imagining what my goose bumps must look like in the firelight. I didn't say anything about lack of body fat, but I thought about it and moved even closer to the fire.

"Get some exercise. The water's warm." Before I could realize what was happening, Harold had hold of my arm and was pulling me toward the pool. Planting my feet firmly, I protested, but two other guys behind me were only too glad to lend Harold a hand.

Suddenly I was flying through the air, stripped of my towel, heading for the water at the deep end of the pool.

"Look out below," Harold called. "Whale launch."

Everyone ooed as I hit the water solidly. I flailed about, then sank straight to the bottom. This proved to be fortunate, because as I hit, I felt my suit top, which I had tied as tightly as possible, get loosened by the water and peel off like the skin slipping off a grape.

Grabbing wildly, I caught it before it slipped over my head and floated away. I twisted and turned at the bottom while I tugged it back in place. Then I surfaced, still holding on to it, in case it wasn't securely tied. Coughing and sputtering, I put my head against the ladder and looked down. It looked all right. Thank goodness. I knew drowning would have been preferable to losing my top altogether.

When I stopped coughing and wheezing, I realized that everyone around me was cheering and clapping. For what? The show, or Harold's trick? Had anyone seen what had really happened? Maybe not—the water was dark. I pretended to cough some more and hid my face again.

"How wonderful to have a friend like Harold." Debra swam over to me. "You okay? I'd say everyone here noticed you, anyway, including you know who."

I sneaked a glance toward the end of the

pool. The trio was sitting on the edge, laughing and talking to the bevy of girls who surrounded them.

"Debra," I whispered. "Didn't you see what happened?"

"Sure. Harold threw you in."

"You didn't see anything else?"

"It took you a long time to come up. I thought I was going to have to go in after you."

"My top came off," I said, gritting my teeth with the effort of keeping the false grin on my face. I was playing the good sport for everyone's eyes. No hard feelings for Harold, the smile said. But I had to know if anyone saw.

"Your what? Really?" Debra started to laugh.

"It wasn't funny." Checking one more time to see that my top was really there, I climbed up the ladder and stepped away from the pool.

"Maggie." Debra followed me. "Oh, Maggie, why do such funny things always happen to you?" She was shaking with laughter.

"I'm just lucky, I guess." I wrapped myself in the towel again, this time determined to go on with the party as if Harold hadn't had his fun.

Debra had hold of Carol by then and was whispering in her ear. Carol's face lit up with glee, I hate to report. She hugged me, but I turned to walk away with as much dignity as I could muster.

"Some friends," I said in a frosty tone of voice and left them to go find some food, safely away from the pool area.

"Hey, Howell." A deep voice behind me interrupted my pout. "Good show."

I turned to find Rob Tyler in line behind me, paper plate and Coke can in hand. He grinned at me, his eyes sparkling flirtatiously.

*Good show?* Speechless, I reached for a hot dog that had just come off the grill. I plopped it on a bun and slathered it with mustard and pickle relish. What did that mean? Could he have seen what else happened? I kept filling my plate with baked beans, potato salad, and another hot dog to stall for time since I knew he was still behind me. If he had . . .

At the end of the line I got up my nerve to say something, but as I turned to speak, I saw him head back to his buddies. I set down my plate, disappointedly. Great timing again, Howell. Now the only thing Rob will remember about me is . . . Just thinking about what happened in the pool made my no-longer-cold body heat up all over, and I knew my cheeks were blazing.

I might never eat again. I would definitely never swim again. *Good show.* Well, one thing was for sure. Rob Tyler had noticed me.

# Chapter 3

The party gave Carol, Debra, and me something to talk about for a week. Other kids talked about it too. Just from rumors and the way new people came up to Carol and acted friendly, I realized the word had spread that Carol had her very own swimming pool. It upped her popularity to about a seven-point-five, at least. And of course, because we were Carol's best friends, we'd see if it did anything for our status as new sophomores at Hammond High. How you get started in a school is so important. Once you're labeled nerd, conceited, or a flirt—any of those negative tags—it's very hard to change your image.

But our images were starting to shape up really great, and even though the possibility of being popular in high school made me nervous, I resolved I'd handle it if it became a reality. Carol was riding high because Dobs Cartwright had been extra friendly when he left the party, and he had spoken to her twice in the hall on Monday and once by her locker on Tuesday. It looked as if exciting things could happen any minute.

What did happen next was something I could never have thought up even in my daydreams.

I'd asked Carol to spend the night on Wednesday, since we had Pep Club meeting after school. Deb, Carol, and I had joined Pep Club. Anyone could be a member. You didn't have to be elected or go through tryouts or anything like you did for cheerleading. We had red sweaters—it took me three baby-sitting jobs to buy mine—and we all sat together at the football games.

We would cheer really loudly to get the whole audience stirred up when our side was behind in the score or to make the team feel good when we were winning. Then during halftime we had card shows. All the cards were red or white and we'd arrange them to spell words about our school or sometimes make pictures.

For two games we were planning to march on the field with the band and make formations. I was part of a bicycle wheel in a special coming up that showed the big sporting events Cedarhurst has. In the summer an important national bike race is held here. Next practice they were going to give out parts for the rest of that show.

It was really proving to be fun, and I was feeling a part of school life right away. There was something about wearing the red sweater that made me feel sort of halfway popular, which of course, I wasn't. After all, school had just started.

I could always count on Mom saying yes to Carol or Debra spending the night even on a school night. I guess she figured she'd know where we were if we were at home. And we had to promise to go to bed early.

Dad had been out of town for two days. He'd

gotten home Wednesday afternoon, starved for home cooking.

"Aren't those jeans a bit tight, Maggie?" he said when Carol and I were helping him do dishes. Even though he'd stuffed himself with roast chicken and mashed potatoes at dinner, he wasn't so full or satisfied that he didn't notice how I looked and what I was wearing.

Usually I'd shrug my shoulders and ignore his remarks, but this time I agreed. "As a matter of fact, they are, Daddy. I guess I've grown this fall."

"Since I brought it up, I suppose that now I have to come up with the money for a new pair." He smiled, and I knew he was in a good mood.

"Well, let's see." I pretended to count on my fingers. "In five weeks, if I give up movies, Cokes, and save really hard, I could afford a pair. But if I grow anymore in that time—"

"I get the idea. But I still can't believe that jeans cost twenty-five dollars. Have you tried Penny's or Sears?"

"Dad . . ." I didn't argue with him, but the tone of my voice said, Surely you know better than that. Carol looked at me and made a face. We loaded the dishwasher and hoped for the best. Mom had gotten the dishwasher fixed with her typing money, so he could probably afford to pay for my new jeans.

"Gee, with you getting so fat, I assume you and Carol don't want to help me make Brownies." Dad was looking in the pantry.

"Daddy, I'm not getting fat. I'm becoming a

woman." I lifted my chin in the air and pretended to be offended by Dad's remark.

"Don't rush it, Maggie. You're going to be my little girl for a long time yet." Dad hugged me and then began rummaging through the cupboard. He set out a Duncan Hines brownie mix on the counter and then casually went off to see what Mom was watching on the TV.

"Wow, for a minute there, I thought he was going to hug me too." Carol read the back of the box while I hunted for a pan.

"Yeah, I know. Isn't it awful? Why can't he realize I haven't been a little girl for years now?"

Sounds of giggles and laughter came from the living room.

"What are they doing?" Carol whispered.

I was a bit embarrassed at having to explain my parents' behavior to anyone, even Carol. "Oh, Dad likes to tickle Mom. Sometimes they really act like kids."

Carol smiled and opened the brownie box. Chocolate smells filled the kitchen. Carol dumped the powder mix into a bowl while I added eggs and water. The mixer whirred while we broke pecans.

"Yum, I don't know if I can wait." Carol scraped the batter, dark brown and gooey, into a square pan, and I pushed it into the preheated oven. She licked the spatula while I dragged my finger around the rim of the bowl.

"Hey, I was going to help." Dad came back in, his face showing mock disappointment.

"I know the way you help, Daddy. You're still in time, though." I handed him the beaters.

"Your mom says I can give you money for jeans." He cleaned off the metal beaters and then licked his fingers.

"Whooppee." I was a bit sarcastic. Had they actually had a family conference over twenty-five dollars? Carol must have ten pairs of jeans and who knows how many dresses, skirts, and sweaters. "Any chance of a shirt too?" No harm asking, I figured.

"Have you outgrown your shirts too?" Dad grinned at that question.

"Oh, no, I probably have at least three I can wear." This time *I* made a face at Carol. Tonight she was getting the picture of why my wardrobe was so limited.

Just then the wall phone in the kitchen jangled, and I figured that would close the discussion. I put the bills Daddy had placed on the kitchen table in my pocket before he or Mom could change their minds. It wasn't like they were poverty-stricken. Dad has a good job as a computer engineer. I think he and Mom made this pact when I was two days old never to spoil me.

"I'll say this for you, Maggie." Carol chewed a piece of ice from her dinner glass of iced tea. (Her dentist probably loves her too.) "You certainly aren't spoiled." She spoke my thoughts exactly.

"You noticed? Well, you know how easy it is to spoil an only child, as they say." I finished putting things in the dishwasher but didn't turn it on till Dad got off the phone.

"Sure. You wouldn't want that to happen."

"No, guess not." Suddenly my mind left the subject of money, clothes, any of my problems. I realized Dad's voice sounded really concerned, and he was saying things like, "When did this happen? Yes, yes, we'll come. Right away."

I looked at his face, which was pulled into a frown, worried, and I started to worry too. "What's wrong, Daddy?"

"Well, your uncle Roger's on the phone. It's Aunt Ruth," he explained. By then Mom had come in the kitchen to see what was going on.

"What's the matter, Dave? What's happened to Ruth?" Mom's face reflected Dad's worry.

My aunt Ruth was Dad's younger sister and a favorite of everyone in the family. She was one of those people who was always laughing, and she kept us all entertained whenever she visited.

"She's having major surgery tomorrow. She went in for a checkup and—"

"Oh, Dave." Mom put her arms around Dad. "We've got to go stay with Roger. Call the airlines. I'll go pack some things. Let's see, I'll have to run a wash. Maggie, can you help me? Maggie . . ." she said again, as if she'd just remembered that I existed. "Oh, Maggie. We can't take you out of school. We might be gone a whole week. You're just getting adjusted to your new school."

"Perhaps she could stay with me, Mrs. Howell," Carol said. "I'll be glad to call my parents and ask."

"Carol, that would be wonderful. Are you sure it wouldn't be an imposition?" Mom looked ready to wring her hands, but even in a crisis like this she always thought of other people.

"I've stayed here several times now. I'm sure I can arrange it." Carol got up from the kitchen table where she'd been sitting listening and headed for the phone.

My heart skipped a beat. While I loved Aunt Ruth dearly and was awfully worried about her myself, a chance to stay with Carol—maybe even for a week—well, I just couldn't believe my good luck. Would her mom say yes? I didn't know anything about Mrs. Barton except that she let Carol do pretty much as she pleased. Surely she would agree, under the circumstances. And I knew they had plenty of room. Why, Mrs. Barton wouldn't even have to know I was there. The house was so big that they had a cook and a maid and a main housekeeper, Hannah, and who knows what other kinds of servants? So it wasn't as if Carol's mom would be put to any trouble.

I moved over close to the phone and raised my eyebrows at Carol questioningly. She put her finger over her lips. "Hannah, it's Carol. Is Mother there?" Carol listened. "When will she be back?" She listened again. "Okay, I'll call back at ten."

I looked at my watch. Two hours. Oh, no. I'd have to suffer for two hours before I would know. The buzzer went off, and I ran to take the brownies out.

"My mother's not home, Mrs. Howell. I'll call her back, but I feel sure I can arrange it. So please don't worry."

*Arrange it?* I had to laugh at Carol's formal language. It sounded like she was planning a safari to Africa instead of just fixing it up for me to spend a few days at her house.

"Maybe I can stay at Debra's if she says no," I said to Carol when Mom and Dad left the room. "But I hope it's okay with your mother." Debra lived in a small trailer south of town. I'd stayed there before, but it was crowded, and we never had much privacy. If I got to go to Carol's, I'd ask her later if Debra could come over for one night. That would be super fun.

It was sheer agony waiting for Mrs. Barton to get home. Carol and I did Mom's laundry, ate more brownies than we should have, played some records, and finally resigned ourselves to doing three pages of algebra on the kitchen table.

We were sitting there when the phone rang again. I answered it. A sophisticated-sounding voice asked if Carol was there. "It's your mom, Carol," I whispered as I held out the phone to her and crossed my fingers.

She rolled her eyes and crossed her fingers too. "Mother, the Howells have an emergency." In her formal, for-parents-only voice she explained the situation. Then she listened for what seemed like a long time. "Yes, Mother," she kept saying. I didn't know what to expect, and Carol wouldn't look at me. She even waved me away once. "All right. Yes, we will. Yes. Yes, you know I will." Finally she hung up.

"Well," I said. "Is it okay?"

"We're in." Carol breathed a sigh of relief. "They're having a formal dinner party one night, and I had to swear we'd make ourselves scarce when the guests are there."

"Oh, we will. She'll never know I'm there, I promise. You can sneak me food, and I'll hide in your closet the whole evening of the party. We're going to have so much fun!" I bounced around the kitchen three times. Gerard went crazy, his toenails clicking on the vinyl in a canine breakdance.

"Oh, no—Gerard. Mom!" I yelled, "what'll we do about Gerard?" I didn't want to have to make a commitment to coming home every day to feed him. That would spoil the whole week.

Mom came in from the bedroom and was relieved to find my housing was taken care of. She had a plan for Gerard by then too. "The Rogers can feed him. I'll pay the kids. Should I have talked to your mother, Carol?"

"Oh, no, ma'am. It's perfectly all right. I owe Maggie about five overnights by now. My mother was perfectly willing after she understood the circumstances."

Mom hugged Carol, and I knew it made Carol uncomfortable, but that was the least of my worries now. "You owe Maggie nothing, Carol," said Mom. "But I really appreciate this. Now I can go off knowing Maggie is well taken care of." Even when she was in the midst of an emergency, Mom couldn't rest until she knew I had a caretaker. When would she trust me enough to let me take care of myself? Maybe by the time I'm forty? I had this vision of going off to my job where I was president of my own company, and Mom was still saying to me, "Are you sure you have a handkerchief, Maggie? And underwear without holes? And your bus fare?"

"Maggie," Mom continued, reaching into her purse. "Here's some money for lunches and any emergencies. I want you to treat Carol to pizza some night." Then she went into a whole list of dos and don'ts and manners and polite guest rules.

I just kept saying yes and nodding my head while I put the cash in my pocket along with the new-jeans money.

Yeaaa! I was out of prison for a few days, maybe even a week. Rich and free! It was too good to be true. Then Gerard jumped up and put his paws on my shoulders, almost knocking me over. He saved me from having to pinch myself.

# Chapter 4

We didn't go to Carol's until after school on Thursday, and by then I was wound up tighter than the dancing monkey I'd gotten for Christmas when I was four, which hopped around clapping cymbals together when you turned it loose.

By sixth-period French class I had daydreamed so much that Miss Peters gave up calling on me to embarrass me back to reality. I guess she finally decided to treat me as though I was absent instead of absentminded. She loved calling on people she suspected weren't prepared. But when she asked me to conjugate *eat* the second time she nailed me, and I said, "Yes, Francine, three chocolate éclairs," she must have realized that the laugh I got made it not worth her while trying again.

Actually I was speaking French during the whole class period. It was to my maid who'd brought me a Pepsi at the pool. I glanced at her over my heart-shaped sunglasses and said "*Merci,* Francine. And for lunch I'll have pizza and three chocolate eclairs, also at the pool, *s'il vous plâit.* I'm not going to move until I finish this novel." The novel was about romance in an exotic country, of course. But I was only reading it to while away the time until I left on my vacation to the French Riviera.

While Carol opened the front door with her key, I turned and drank in the view. The lawn, which sloped gently downhill, was dotted with pines and blue spruce. A maple near the door blazed in a showoff shade of maroon, and a few of the brilliant leaves had drifted onto the redstone patio.

"What's this?" I pointed to what looked like a small computer near the massive oak door.

"Burglar alarm," Carol said, juggling her books and flute case. "New one. Someone got past the first one we had. It's not activated right now, though, or I'd have to turn it off quickly."

"A burglar alarm?" I laughed. "Nobody would want to steal anything at my place. And if they tried, Gerard would lick them to death."

We walked down a hall that was practically the entire length of my house. Rooms led off of it in all directions—big rooms with cathedral ceilings and skylights. There was a huge moss-rock fireplace in one—the living room, I guessed—and Indian rugs hung everywhere.

"My dad likes Indian stuff."

"I can see that. It looks like a museum in here. I hope you have a map handy so you can find your way to your room." I shifted books to my other arm.

"When we first moved here, I used a ball of string. I had to. Felicity kept eating the bread crumbs I dropped behind me." Carol started up a flight of stairs that was so wide two cars could have passed each other with ease.

By Felicity I assumed Carol meant the ani-
mated ball of fluff who bounded toward us,
blue eyes questioning whether or not we were
to be permitted in her house. Then she wove
herself around and between my legs all the way
to the top of the stairs.

"Mom has three Persians. One is so old,
though, that she can't walk anymore: we have to
carry her from chair to chair. All she does is
sleep and watch the world go by."

I stopped at the door to Carol's room, feeling
sort of afraid to go in. It was twice the size of
mine, but that wasn't what intimidated me. There
wasn't a pillow out of place. The yellow shag
rugs looked as if no one had ever set foot on
them. Custard-colored curtains ruffled along-
side the windows. A wall cabinet with a stereo
and about a thousand records was practically
the only evidence that someone actually lived
there. There was a portable TV and a VCR on
the same shelf, along with a few books. On the
bed three stuffed animals—a lion, a tiger, and a
leopard—looked as though they were afraid to
move. Just seeing the outside of Carol's house
had led me to expect a lot from the inside, but
this was more than my imagination could have
ever come up with.

"Are you competing for a spread in *House
Beautiful* or will you be willing to just settle for a
clean-teen-of-the-year award?" All of a sudden
I felt kind of awkward and ill at ease with Carol.
I guess my voice betrayed how I felt.

Carol sensed it immediately. "Maggie, don't
act so weird. Come on in. I keep my room this

clean so Hannah will stay out; even so, I suspect she sneaks in during the day and dusts or straightens out the hangers in the closet."

The image of Hannah dusting hangers relaxed me a little, making me smile on the inside. "How can you live in here?" The cat jumped on the bed and stared at me. She knew she belonged here, and I suspect she knew that I didn't.

"Very carefully. Here's your suitcase. Your mom and dad dropped it off before they left. They must have gotten off all right. Put it in the closet after you unpack. You can have this drawer and the left side of the closet."

It sounded as if Carol expected me to be a neat freak too while I was here. Oh, well, when in Rome ... For a minute I had panicked, thinking that Mom had forgotten to bring over my cosmetic case. Not that it was full of cosmetics, but it had my pajamas and lots of other essential junk in it. I shoved stuff into the drawer Carol indicated and then headed for the closet. Oh, boy. It was as big as Debra's whole bedroom. Wait till she saw this! She'd either flip out or move in. She could live in here with all the clothes and Carol would never know. Let's see, bed under the sweater shelf ... I peeked out to see where Carol was, then swung around and did a quick calculation. I couldn't help it. Eight, ten, sixteen, nineteen sweaters. All lined up in a row like at Fashion Bar, except these were all one size. Perfect. Geez, I'm glad she's already seen my humble room. Otherwise I'd have to have told her I was a runaway and lived at the bus station.

"Not a bad setup, Carol. For starters." I sat carefully in a rocking chair after first checking the seat for the ancient feline. I definitely did not want to squash her mother's most cherished antique.

"It'll do." Carol had flopped on the bed, seemingly unconcerned that she was wrinkling it. "Want a Tab?" she finally said after a few minutes of unaccustomed silence between us. When she looked at me, her eyes had kind of a pleading look in them. So I tried to act naturally.

"How far away is the kitchen? Would we be back in time for the six o'clock news? I gotta watch it. I have a crush on Tom Brokaw." Actually I was content just to sit there and observe how the other half lived. I felt a little like the breath had been knocked out of me.

"One-two-three-five steps." Carol smiled and watched for the look on my face as she hopped up and pushed a button on what I thought was probably a wall safe holding her Beatles collection. The door swung open to reveal a mini-refrigerator, stocked with soda, juice, and milk.

"Ah . . . yes. I'll just have R C on the rocks with a twist of lemon, Perkins. Be sure it's at least thirty-nine degrees Fahrenheit. I hate warm cola." I was acting extra silly and starting to regain my sense of humor. After all, it was still the same old Carol—I hoped.

"You're too much, Maggie. I should have known I could count on you to take all this in stride." Carol handed me a plain Coke. I hated diet drinks.

"Is that why you've never invited me here? Were you afraid I'd be impressed? I'm impressed, I'm impressed."

"Well, I wanted you to get to know the real me first."

"The real you. Yes. The one with the nineteen sweaters and a chauffeur to drive you to school. Will the real Carol Barton please stand up? Is it the one in the ragged jeans, longing to live in a commune in the Rocky Mountains? The one with the dust-buster in hand, defending her room from Hannah? Or the plain, everyday fifteen-year-old who graces Hammond High with her presence?"

"Come on, Maggie. Let's talk about boys or something, or I'll pour this ice down your sweat shirt. You've had your fun with my life-style. Get real."

"What's real is that I'm finally here." Something about the tone of Carol's voice made me want to get up and hug her. I didn't of course. "Can you believe it?"

"Sure. It was just a matter of time. You want to have a swim before dinner?" Carol started looking through a drawer trying to decide which bathing suit to wear.

I took a sip of Coke to hide my smile. "Real" for Carol was swimming before dinner, hot-tubbing at bedtime, what else? I could hardly wait to find out what it was like now that my initial shock was fading.

\*　　\*　　\*

I had some things to learn, I discovered. After our swim we dried our hair at the pool house, and I put my sweats back on. But I found out I couldn't wear them to dinner.

"Why not?" I asked when Carol told me. "What's wrong with rust-colored sweats? They match my long, flowing auburn hair." I lounged (carefully) on Carol's bed like Cleo on her barge, pretending that the pillows were made of knitted llama hair and the stuffed lion was real.

"Come on, hurry up." Carol looked at her watch. "What else did you bring?" She headed for the closet.

I got up, reluctantly. We'd swum a lot of laps, and I felt positively languid. No, languorous. I rolled each word over deliciously in my mouth. Both sounded decadent. I was going to love practicing hedonism and decadence all week long. It might be the only chance I ever got. And I am definitely one to want to experience the world in all its diversity.

"Maggie," Carol called from the closet, "all you have are jeans and sweats. Didn't you even bring one skirt and blouse?"

"Let's see. I think I had a skirt two years ago, but—"

"Here." Carol threw a skirt at me. "I have this one that's the new super-long style. You're thinner than I am, but you can wear this top that hangs over the waist. It disguises the inch I can pinch."

I got up and wriggled into the gathered black skirt—not my color, but it couldn't be helped. Fortunately the top was turquoise, one of my best colors. "It's your fault, Carol. You didn't tell me we had to *dress* for dinner."

"Here, try these." Carol stood in front of a jewelry box that was nearly as large as my overnight case. She tossed a pair of earrings at me— *dangling* earrings. "And hurry up."

The long turquoise and silver dangles were wonderful. I looked just as sexy as I'd imagined I would. What if I got used to this way of dressing in a week, this way of living, this decadence? Could I go back? Can Magnolia Howell return to the roots that nourished her but left her feeling unfulfilled as a woman?

"Come *on*, Maggie." Carol stood in the doorway with her hands on her hips. "The mirror will still be there when we get back."

"Newly Windexed," I murmured, but Carol ignored me. I bounded down the stairs behind her until she came to an abrupt halt at a wide double door. She took a deep breath as if preparing for a stage entrance, straightened her shoulders, and glided—yes, glided—into a dining room that would rival a set for "Destinies."

Mirrors up and down each wall reflected the light from two chandeliers, crystal of course, overhead and at each end of the table. The table was about eight feet long. Mr. and Mrs. Barton sat at either end. Carol and I were obviously supposed to sit in the middle opposite each other, since two places were laid with enough silver to mint next year's coins. Hannah stood waiting—to do what?—pull a bell cord to tell the cook the delinquents had arrived?

Mrs. Barton, a blond woman whose hair color

must come from a fifty-dollar trip to the beauty shop twice a month, raised her arm and motioned me to her left. I didn't realize I'd stopped, frozen, at the dining-room door. Carol was waiting for me to follow her. Mrs. Barton had on one of those flowing caftans you see in *Vogue* or *Harper's Bazaar,* jet black, with this year's style of batwing sleeves. I couldn't have been any more startled had she been hanging upside down from the chandelier, staring at me.

"Carol, do sit down. We've been waiting. Is this your little friend?"

Carol's little friend finally got to her chair, then remembered to close her mouth. What was I supposed to do next?

# Chapter 5

I almost panicked as I looked from Mrs. Barton to Mr. Barton. He wore a dark suit and a tie. Dear Miss Manners: What do you say to Bat Lady after you've been introduced and whispered, "Pleased to meet you." I guess—I hoped I was pleased to meet Carol's mother. Time would tell. Mr. Barton nodded at me but seemed preoccupied with something. I figured that it wasn't the electric bill. My dad is always saying, "Turn off the lights when you leave a room, Maggie. I don't own stock in the electric company, you know." I was willing to bet Mr. Barton did.

Finally I realized I wasn't expected to say anything else. I relaxed a little, looked at Carol, who made a face but picked up the outside spoon for her soup. She showed it to me. I did the same. As I sipped, very carefully, the clear broth that tasted of lemon, I listened for a minute to the conversation that bounced back and forth from one end of the table to the other.

I don't know why I do this, but a thought came to me that almost made me choke on a grain of rice. Maybe it had to do with the length of the table. Suddenly I had this picture of Mr. and Mrs. Barton holding cans to their ears with a string attaching them, like we did when we were kids, pretending we had our own phones.

"Did Harris finally decide to plea-bargain that case, Hubert?"

"No, but I'm sure he will. It no longer concerns me."

"The Stetwilers will be at the dinner party Friday night. You wanted to talk to him, remember?"

"There's a voter's meeting in Longmont, but I've told them it's important to know I have Burt Stetwiler's support. That's a strategic invitation."

Strategic? Were they discussing a battle or a dinner party? Back and forth, back and forth, and for a minute I followed the formal speeches as I would the ball in a tennis match. Then I decided I must look foolish swiveling my head like an owl. Didn't they ever speak to Carol at dinner?

Finally Mr. Barton turned to her. "Carol, have you gotten your report card for the quarter?"

"No, sir," Carol replied, and then I realized where she had learned that for-parents-only voice. "But I expect three As and two Bs."

"What subjects are you making Bs in?" Mr. Barton pushed away his empty soup bowl and focused his whole attention on Carol. I could see a cross-examination coming. "And where were you when the As were being handed out?"

"History and algebra." Carol confessed to her crime rather than be grilled.

"Do you need a tutor for the math class?" Hubert Barton, attorney, continued.

A tutor? He had to be kidding. When Carol was getting a B? I couldn't believe it. I was getting an A in math, but just barely. I had expected a B+ since I'd missed one exam, but Mrs. Cazort, our teacher, was very fair. I had been sick, so she'd written up a completely new exam for me and then let me take it home and do it overnight.

"No thank you, Father. I think I'm catching on. I'm sure I can raise that B to an A by the end of the semester."

"The colleges look at more than grades. Don't you think so, Maggie?" Mrs. Barton brushed a curl back up into her swept-up hairdo and re-fastened a comb. I was glad to see that her style wasn't totally spray-painted in place as I'd thought. "That's why we gave you flute lessons—to help you be more well rounded. You must join some other organizations besides Pep Club. Some with substance."

"They're trying to get the Photography Club started again. That might be fun," I suggested. Then I wished I had kept still. Even though Mrs. Barton had asked my opinion, I guess she hadn't really expected an answer. Both of them looked at me as if *fun* were a four-letter word and not proper at the dining table.

"I had thought more along the lines of Debate, or perhaps some of the science clubs." Mrs. Barton leaned back to let Hannah take her soup bowl. "Then if you want to run for a class office, dear, your father's campaign manager can get you some posters printed."

"I'll think about it," Carol promised. And that

seemed to end her part in the evening's conversation. An uncomfortable silence descended on the table, as if no one knew anything else to say.

"Are your parents going to the dance next weekend?" Mrs. Barton finally asked me.

Dance? What dance? I wondered.

"I don't think they belong to the club," Mr. Barton told his wife. "I haven't met them yet."

Oh, the country club. I'd heard my father's opinion of country clubs, but I doubted it would go over big in this conversation. Obviously they expected me to say something now, though. "My parents like to square-dance. They belong to the Star Prowlers."

I knew the Star Prowlers wasn't in the same social category as the Cedarhurst Country Club, but my mom and dad really loved to square-dance. Sometimes they went two or three times a week when they weren't working so hard. They'd do a warm-up spin or two in the living room while Gerard barked. Mom would twirl her full skirts and petticoats to reveal a sexy garter. They'd laugh and Dad would kiss her before they left.

The Bartons had no opinion they could express politely about square dancing, so it got quiet again. What we needed was a dog or a two-year-old to liven up the dinner hour.

Speaking of kids, where was Carol's little brother? Was there a rule that you had to be over the milk-spilling age to take part in the family dinner hour?

I had my answer by the time the grilled sole arrived. Hannah brought Sam in to say good night to his parents. It was a relief to see the mischievous look in his eyes and his tousled mop of blond hair that said, normal, bratty five-year-old. But he was well trained too. On his best behavior, he walked to each parent for a good-night kiss.

"Why are you wearing Carol's new sweater?" he said to me when Carol introduced me to him.

Caught. Uh-oh. "Girls think it's fun to trade clothes," I said without thinking. I'd used that word again, but this time it seemed to go unnoticed.

Hannah swept Sam out as quickly as she'd ushered him in. He was off the hook for the evening. I wished I could have escaped with him. Especially when Mr. and Mrs. Barton got into a disagreement about another engagement for Saturday night and the air got frosty.

I concentrated on eating my fish before it got cold. I wished I could have had seconds of the little potatoes mixed with peas and some kind of sauce. But the portions were already on the plates when they came in, and I guessed no one ever asked for more.

Mrs. Barton left her plate half full when the main course was finished. Was she on a diet, or had the disagreement with Mr. Barton made her lose her appetite?

Dessert was a fancy molded thing of chocolate pudding, ice cream, and nuts. While I licked my spoon and quietly scraped every bit of the delicious concoction from my plate, I glanced over to see if Carol's mother would leave half of her dessert too. To my dismay, after about two bites, she sent practically the whole thing back to the kitchen. I wondered if Hannah, or whoever washed dishes, needed help putting away leftovers.

Oh, well, maybe Carol and I could sneak back downstairs later and check out the kitchen. Mr. and Mrs. Barton had coffee and something amber colored in little tiny glasses. Was it sherry? A liqueur? "I'll just have a liqueur with my coffee, Perkins." I pictured myself in a champagne-colored gown with a brown boa. Perkins would bow and say, "Very well, madame. I'll get it right away." I knew they had drinks before dinner, during dinner, and after dinner in movies and books, but I'd never seen it really happen. My parents opened a bottle of wine for Christmas and New Year's. Sometimes on birthdays, but not every night.

Carol kicked me under the table. "May we be excused, Father? We have some homework to do." She waited politely for permission.

"Thank you for a delightful dinner," I said to both parents when our parole was granted. Why should I thank them? Someone else had cooked it. Hannah had served it. But then I guess Mr. Barton paid the grocery bill, and Carol had set the tone for exiting the room. Far be it from me to commit a *faux pas* now.

"Whew, do you have to do that every evening, Carol?" I said as we ran back up the stairs.

"Do what? Eat? Of course."

I was referring to the ordeal, but I guess Carol was used to it. She must think we're real slobs at our house, and I'm sure her mom doesn't hurry off to her room to finish typing a romance for someone. Mrs. Barton could have stepped out of one of those stuffy English novels herself, but I didn't really detect any romantic overtones in her conversation with "Hubert." Maybe it was a marriage of convenience.

"May I kiss you good night, dear?" Hubert would say.

"Of course, dear, but don't muss my hair or spill your liqueur on my batwings." Mrs. Barton would tilt up her beautifully chiseled face, receive her peck on the cheek, and smile prettily.

I tucked Carol's parents into the back of my mind with that scenario and hunted up my algebra book. We did study when we got back to Carol's room—a sanctuary, I now realized, its spotless appearance notwithstanding. I sat on the floor on one side of the bed, using a worn corduroy backrest with arms that Carol kept hidden in her closet. She said her mother would think it was too grubby and would throw it out if she found it. Carol worked at her desk. A stack of records changed automatically, so it didn't get so quiet we couldn't think.

Math seemed easy for me so far, so I was able to help Carol with a couple of algebra problems. Maybe I could apply for the job of tutor and increase my spending money if Mr. Barton kept insisting that Carol get help.

Then I started thinking about how maybe I could help Rob Tyler with his algebra too. I'd noticed he wasn't exactly great at it. I wondered why he hadn't taken algebra in his sophomore year like most kids had. Not that I'm complaining. It's so great to have a class with him.

Carol helped me conjugate some French verbs, so I ended up thinking the barter system would work better for us than if her parents paid me as a tutor. When I get to France, I want to be able to speak the language. French is such a sexy language and I have a lot of fun trying to speak it. What Carol has is a natural talent for imitating—she sounds so sophisticated when Miss Peters calls on her in class. She will probably get to Paris and the Riviera before I do, but I'll keep daydreaming and wishing and planning anyway.

"If a handsome Parisian falls in love with you, Carol, can I come visit you in your apartment overlooking the Seine?"

"What?" Carol spun around and looked at me funny. She hadn't been following my fantasy, of course. "Is your mind ever in Cedarhurst, USA, Maggie? You have logged so many miles on your flights of fantasy that you are probably eligible for one of United's free tickets to anywhere."

"Oh, I hope so. I'd hate to think I was working this hard only to be able to prepare a *petit déjeuner* for my husband and six kids."

"If you have six kids, the breakfast won't be *petit.*"

We laughed, mostly at the idea of either of us having six kids. Thank goodness zero population growth is what society seems to approve of these days.

"I'm hungry," I announced. "Let's go see if

there's any of that dessert left, or make some fudge." I was sure that Carol's kitchen would be well supplied so that there would be ingredients for any occasion.

"Oh, Maggie. We can't. Nadia would kill me if I messed up her kitchen. That's why I have my own fridge. I never use any of the kitchen supplies unless it's to restock my drink supply."

The idea of never going into the kitchen at night seemed as foreign to me as being in Paris or London. I stood up and opened the door to Carol's refrigerator. I held it open as long as I wanted to; there was no one here to say, "Shut the door, Maggie. You're wasting electricity." Trouble was, it took only ten seconds to see that Carol had nothing left except diet soda. And the tiny freezer was as bare as the Arctic Circle.

"We can stop to get some Häagen-Dazs after school tomorrow." Carol apologized for having no snacks.

"But that's almost twenty hours away," I moaned. "When I start to think about food, I can't stop." I grabbed my purse from the stack of books I'd dragged from school, just in case I got desperate enough to do homework. Digging to the bottom, I came up with two breath mints. How could I have let it get so empty? Usually I had at least some Dum-Dums or part of a candy bar. After all, what if I got trapped in an elevator, or locked in the girls' bathroom for three hours by accident?

"Okay, now I remember that you are a bottomless pit." Carol looked around. "But I didn't have much time to prepare for your visit, remember? If I'd had more advanced warning, I'd have bought out half of Safeway's snack aisles. You eat more than any friend I ever had who is so skinny." Carol didn't seem to mind that she weighed about twenty pounds more than I did. She was just stating a fact.

"It's a mixed blessing. Can't we do anything?" I was about to start pacing the floor and wringing my hands.

"The house is locked up by now." Carol looked at her watch. "Wait, I just remembered." She walked into her closet. I followed and watched as she opened a cupboard on the side and started to dig. *"Voilà!* Hannah gave me this popcorn popper for Christmas last year. I'd forgotten."

"Forgotten? How could you?" I grabbed it out of her hands. "You do have oil and corn, don't you? Please don't tell me you don't."

"Does it get stale?" Carol came back to her room from the closet with three-quarters of a jar of Orville's kernels.

"Who cares? I'm desperate." I snatched the jar from her and soon had the lid of the popper bouncing. I huddled over it. A watched popper . . . "Good thing I don't like butter on it."

Carol shook her head in dismay as I emptied out the fluffy kernels and started stuffing my face. "A high rate of metabolism in some teenage girls, naming no names, should be against some rule of nature. Or at least be banned by a state ordinance." She took a small handful.

"Sorry." I leaned back, starting to feel as though I might survive, after all. "I guess for a few minutes there I panicked."

"I noticed." Carol got out her pajamas.

I wondered how far her room was from her parents'. With no one to tell us to be quiet and go to bed, I was tempted to sit up half the night talking. But common sense finally prevailed. One, I knew I'd get hungry again in a couple of hours if I wasn't asleep. And two, my eight o'clock class in biology was hard enough even when I'd had enough sleep. Also Friday was pop-quiz day. It would be just like Mr. Quiz-en-art, as we called our biology teacher, to ask us to name all the inhabitants of the Mesozoic era.

While I saw little in my future that would depend on my reciting those facts to get a job, half our final grade rested on the scores of pop quizzes. My parents weren't as hard on me about grades as Carol's seemed to be, but I did plan to go to the state university and I knew I'd have to have good marks to get in.

It felt funny to wake up without Gerard's barking and dancing and licking—even funnier to wake up in Carol's bedroom. She had switched on her TV, and we watched the early news and the first part of "Good Morning, America" while we got dressed. I fumbled around until I got my jeans on, wishing I could wear one of Carol's sweaters. But she didn't offer, and I hated to ask. She probably never realized that having me in her closet was like turning a baby loose in a candy store. I had to settle for the purple blouse that everyone at school had seen at least two dozen times this year. Mom had told me to get a more neutral color that people wouldn't recognize every time, but I just had to have purple. I hated it when her taste in clothes always proved to be right, but if I could just have more variety in my wardrobe, it wouldn't be so much of a problem.

Down in the kitchen Hannah was watching the "Today" show while she drank a cup of coffee and supervised Sam's demolition of his oatmeal. He had mixed in raisins, maple syrup, and peanuts by the time I couldn't bear to watch anymore. Not that different from a Granola bar, I supposed.

"Where are your mom and dad?" I asked as Paul Newman appeared on the screen. He was talking about selling peanut butter or salad dressing, or something like that. I couldn't get past his blue eyes to remember the product or even care about it. I thought it was kind of a funny thing for him to be doing, though. Paul Newman's peanut butter? No. I just couldn't associate peanut butter with his sexy image.

"Dad's gone to work, I guess." Carol reached for a second piece of toast to munch on with her grapefruit half. I was glad I'd been able to order bacon, two eggs, and a sweet roll. "Mom hardly ever appears till about ten."

"Who nags you to be careful and asks if you have everything?" The sweet roll was homemade and full of cinnamon and almond slices. I licked my fingers until Hannah took the hint and brought me another one.

Carol laughed. "Hannah used to. Now I have to make my own lists."

"Oh." I pretended to read my list. "Don't

wear that scarf like that, Maggie, it looks tacky. Don't forget your French homework. Don't forget to stop and get Häagen-Dazs for a snack tonight. Try Rocky Road this time." I mopped the last of my soft-boiled egg with the corner of a sweet bite of pastry. While it was nice not to have to be so formal about my food, I was used to having someone say, "Have a good day."

No one said anything as we went out the back door and down to the garage where Charles had a car waiting to take us to school. For a minute I wondered about Aunt Ruth. Today was her surgery. I hoped Mom would call me tonight.

Then I got totally distracted by sitting in the back of the Mercedes and being driven to school. Charles stopped at the corner, two blocks from Hammond High, and I realized Carol was getting out. I scooted across the leather seat and followed her while Charles held the door.

"Thanks, Charles. Have a good day."

He seemed startled that I'd spoken to him, but he smiled, nodded, and then got back into the driver's seat and left.

"Do you always do that?" I skipped to catch up with Carol, who had hurried away from the car.

"What?" She slowed up. She must know what I meant.

"Get off two blocks from school?"

"Of course. How would it look if I arrived at the front door every day with Charles driving me?"

"Too-too." I posed like a svelte model.

"Exactly." Carol walked on up the hill ahead of me. Was she mad at me? What had I done, except find out what her real world was like? It didn't mean I liked her less for it. And although the way she lived was one hundred and eighty degrees away from my life-style, having money wasn't exactly the worst thing that could happen to a person.

Debra and I had PE third period while Carol took music. I could hardly wait to fill her in on the details we'd wondered about so many times when we were alone. But I also had to figure out a way to get her inside Carol's house so she could see for herself. Maybe since Carol's mother had lowered her standards enough to let me visit, she would make an exception for one more of Carol's impoverished friends.

# Chapter 6

"Carol, wait up." I ran after Carol and then had to stop to catch my breath before I could make my suggestion. "Listen. Let's get Debra to come over tonight. We can go shopping at the mall for my jeans, and I'll buy you pizza as Mom suggested. Your mom and dad will be throwing that dinner party, remember? Your mom won't even have to know your guests have increased by one, will she?"

"I might be able to get away with it." Carol considered my suggestion. "It's better if I ask before I have anybody over, though."

"Don't worry. Debra can leave tomorrow before your mom gets up. And if you call Hannah, we can just take the bus to the mall after school. She won't have to fix us dinner, and we can get back to your place when the party is in full swing and your parents won't even notice." Given the size of Carol's house, I would think she could have a slumber party of at least ten kids in her room and no one would ever know. That is, if we made sure to clean up afterward.

"I'll think about it," Carol promised as we took our seats in Mr. Wisenhart's biology classroom.

I kept looking forward to the evening, feeling

pretty sure I could talk Carol into it. If I had all the freedom that Carol had with her parents going to meetings and dinner parties and doing that political stuff all the time, I would be much more creative. As far as I could see, the only thing Carol did with her free time was to spend it at my house where we had all these dumb rules about administering the rules.

Then Quiz-en-art interrupted my fun and pulled out the "little test he knew we would all enjoy." If his pop quizzes were really surprises, most of the class would probably flunk. But he'd made such a habit of giving them that the brains had caught on and started to prepare for them, and that put pressure on us all.

Halfway through the exam, a piece of folded paper bounced at my feet. I glanced at Mr. Wisenhart. I really think he gave the Friday tests so he had time to plan his weekend. As we scribbled away furiously, he leaned back in his chair and studied a copy of *Denver Today*, which listed all the movies, art shows, plays, music, and restaurants the big city had to offer. To me, Cedarhurst offered more than any one person could ever get around to doing, but I did know lots of people who drove to Denver all the time.

I dropped my pencil, then scooped up the note at the same time that I retrieved it. "What's up?" it said, and there was a smile face with question marks all around the head. "Let's do something tonight." Debra knew I had gone to Carol's after school yesterday. In fact, I'm sure she got sick of my mentioning it all day long.

"Tell you third period," I scribbled on the back of the note, then walked over to sharpen my pencil, making sure I passed in front of Deb's desk.

Harold Tubbs saw the whole exchange and smiled at me on the way back. Then he scraped one finger on top of the other to say, "Naughty, naughty."

What was it about me that held a fascination for the nerds of the world? Maybe it was that I just didn't have it in me to say with words, or body English, or whatever, "Get lost, creep." It must be that I was just low enough down on the social totem pole myself to have sympathy with those who were really at the bottom. The way that I looked at it was that you had to be in the top ten to risk offending *anyone*. But then could a girl like Hilary Harlow, who was the current number one, even have an inkling of what it was like to be me, much less to be someone at the very bottom of society?

All those self-help books on being number one were lost on me. I think when I grow up I'll write a book called, *Being in the Middle and Accepting It If Not Just Downright Enjoying It. The View from the Middle of the Stairs.* That was me. I could see the falseness of being number one— and the miserableness of being number three hundred.

I could also see me being grounded for three years if I flunked biology. So I tried to get my mind back to what was truly meaningful about the Mesozoic era. It was the age of gymnosperms and cycads. Wow, how had I lived this long without knowing that? At least I'd guessed right about the subject matter of today's quiz. And I had even studied for a few minutes.

Watching Rob Tyler got me through algebra without dying of boredom; and then, lo and behold, he stopped me after class.

"Hey, Maggie. Think you can do tomorrow's assignment or do you need help?" Rob smiled and made me feel like I'd be glad to take all the help from him I could get. I hated girls who pretended to be dumb in front of boys, though.

"Depends on who volunteers for the tutoring." Wow, did I say that? I was actually flirting. Please, please don't let my face turn red.

"To tell the truth, Maggie, I'm the one who needs help. I notice you're not having any trouble in this class."

I was having more trouble than he knew—trouble keeping my eyes off him and on the blackboard. "I'd be glad to help you, Rob," I said. Might as well be honest. "Just let me know when."

"Thanks, Maggie. I will." He took off without making any specific plans. Was he serious? He sounded serious.

Carol and Debra had waited for me, and as Debra and I left Carol to run to dress for PE, she whispered, "Progress?"

I smiled. "Progress. I think."

I sure hope so, I thought, as I slipped out of my street clothes and into my shorts and gym shirt. Lucky Carol with her flute lesson to have her PE requirement out of the way early and not to have to change clothes and get all sweaty halfway through the day. I wasn't very musical, though, so playing a flute sounded like work to me too.

I filled Debra in on Rob and the view from the top of the economic strata in Cedarhurst while we chased the volleyball around the gym. The idea was to hit it over the net, but I did more chasing than hitting. Debra was pretty athletic and really graceful. Miss Almanrode told us to hush twice, but fortunately she's pretty relaxed about her class and didn't give us detention. Debra liked my idea of sneaking into Carol's room, and by two-thirty we had Carol talked into calling Hannah.

"What did she say?" I asked as soon as Carol hung up the pay phone outside the front of school.

"That it was a good idea. I'd be out of the way." Carol picked up her tote bag. Even on the weekend she took books home. If I was expected to get straight As, I would too. But today I had all my homework done. I only had my French book, and that was because I wanted to take advantage of extra time speaking the language with Carol. She always laughed at my pronunciation, but I knew I could get it right if I heard it often enough. Just speaking in class wasn't enough.

"Hannah probably has to help your mom get dressed," I said in case Carol felt bad about Hannah suggesting she was in the way at home. Someone must help Mrs. Barton fix those hairdos. Unless she'd spent the afternoon at the beauty shop. You could do that if you were going out or if someone else was cooking dinner. Not to mention the big bucks it must cost to stay beautiful as you got older. I'd settle for a new mascara wand. I wondered how much of my emergency money I dared spend.

I tried on about six pairs of jeans before we ended up at the Limited. They had Forenza imports if I could afford a pair or they happened to be on sale. They were stylishly faded, and everyone was wearing them this year. Carol had a Visa card, and obviously no one questioned her spending money on clothes.

Even if we didn't buy anything, it was *the* place to be seen. The jeans were on sale, but we tried on half the things in the store before we chose. There were three junior girls in the store. They were in the Pep Club with us, and apparently just being in the same store with them gave us some status. They stopped to talk, and they'd never done that at school.

"Dobs Cartwright asked me if I knew you, Carol," Mary Fern Davidson whispered to Carol. Of course we could all hear her, so she didn't mean it to be a secret. "I think he likes you. Maybe you should even start looking for a dress for the homecoming dance."

Maybe Debra and I were on our way to being tugged into the top ten in the sophomore class on Carol's shirttails. I guess it was better than not being accepted at all, and at least I'd get some experience.

What I really wondered was what Mary Fern and Helen Redgraves would think if they saw Carol coming to school in a Mercedes? It was not something to be ashamed of. Maybe I could instruct Charles to drive us right up to the door on Monday.

*I* could pull it off. "Thank you so much, Charles"—the English pronunciation. "And I won't need you anymore today. Dobs Cartwright will see that I get home safely."

I paid cash for the jeans, and Carol charged two tops. Then we walked over to Taco Express. They have the best nachos in town—super nachos, they're called, and they're served with a big glob of guacamole and another of sour cream. I had this secret plan of buying one extra serving to sneak into Carol's place for midnight snacking. Now that I knew the circumstances of Carol's kitchen being off limits, I'd end up being better prepared before I went back to her house.

Debra's mom had said she could spend the night with us when she called home, so now all we had to do was sneak her in. For all I knew Mrs. Barton might have said it was fine for Debra to stay over if Carol had asked her instead of asking Hannah. But the *idea* of sneaking Debra in was so much fun I didn't want to give it up.

While we waited for our food to come, I'd gone to the phone booth in the hall and called Aunt Ruth's, charging it with my parents' card. It was nice to talk to Mom.

Aunt Ruth had gotten through the surgery fine, and things looked good for her recovery. I felt a lot better and told Mom I'd been worried.

I didn't want her to think I didn't care, or was having such fun that I'd forgotten.

"When will you be here?" I asked. Not too soon, I hoped, crossing my fingers.

"Are you all right at Carol's?"

"Sure, Mom. Fine. No one even notices me there, her place is so big."

"Well, then, we may stay through the week since we've spent so much getting here. And Roger needs us. Ruth won't come home for several days, and then she'll have to stay in bed."

"No problem," I assured her. "We're not bothering anyone here."

"I miss you," Mom said. " 'Bye, love you."

"Love you too." I hung up and stood there for a minute. I did miss them a little, but it was because I didn't leave home very often. Neither did they. I had gone to camp, but somehow that was different.

"Good news," I announced when I got back to our table. "It looks as though they may stay all week. Think I can stay with you that long, Carol?"

"Sure. Now that you're there, it's okay. You could have stayed over before, but I was being silly about trusting you."

I still felt kind of bad that Carol hadn't thought it would be okay before. Imagine someone not wanting you to see where she lives because it's so incredibly posh. I was still smiling over the idea when our food arrived. The guy that brought it over smiled back at me.

"Hey, how come you're so popular all of a sudden?" Debra demanded to know.

"My dad always told me a smile does wonders for your personality. I'm beginning to think he's right." I lifted a taco chip, dribbling the guacamole all over my fingers. "Maybe we don't give parents enough credit. Ten percent of what they tell us may just be right."

"Yeah, but it's exhausting to have to listen to the other ninety percent." Debra licked the sour cream off her bite.

We laughed and talked and ate and planned the rest of the evening. I was so glad we'd had this idea. I love being with either Carol or Debra alone, but the three of us together are dynamite.

We figured we'd sneak in the back door and up the backstairs. Then if the coast was clear, we'd sneak out to the pool and go swimming tomorrow morning before Debra had to go home. The Indian summer days had lingered on, and temperatures were still in the seventies every day. It would be fun to try to keep our tans till almost Christmas.

"Let's just take the bus home," said Carol, shifting her heavy tote to her other hand when we got outside Taco Express. "I don't feel like calling Charles."

It took two transfers, but we had lots to talk about, so the extra time didn't matter. The bus stopped right behind Carol's house, and it was easy to run up the grassy slope to the back entrance.

"So far, so good," Carol whispered. She was getting into the swing of things at last. She seemed so tense when I had asked to bring Debra. Maybe she didn't trust Debra to see her layout any more than she had me. Gee, what was the worst her mom could do if she found Carol had an extra guest? Take away her credit card? I had never known Carol to be grounded since school had started. A couple of years ago it had seemed that I spent most of my life grounded, but something had changed. Either I'd gotten smarter or I was conforming more to parental standards of teen behavior. I often wondered what the rules would be if teens set the rules for teens. Every bit as tough, maybe, but more reasonable.

Just as I'd figured, we could have slipped the whole pep squad up the back stairs. We didn't see a soul until we reached Carol's room.

"Sam, what are you doing in my room?" Carol asked, dumping her books on the floor, forgetting the uncluttered look she usually strove for. Of course, Sam had already messed things up anyway. He was eating potato chips, drinking soda, and watching Carol's TV.

"I'm recording on mine." He didn't move.

"On both channels?" She picked up the empty chip bag and Sam's soda can.

"No, but I wanted to record this too if it was good." Sam stood up. He knew he was about to be ejected.

"Go watch it on Hannah's TV." Carol punched the off button for the VCR and flipped the channel to "Destinies," which was just coming on.

Sam stopped in the doorway. "How come you

only told Mother you have one guest, and now you have two?"

"Sam, it doesn't matter. Just get out." Carol sank onto the floor. "You guys don't know what you're missing, not having a little brother."

"I don't mind. Hey, watch out, Debra. That isn't a pillow in Carol's rocker." I pointed to the old cat, who lay there curled up in a ball, purring loudly. "How'd she get in here?"

"That's Maud. Sam probably carried her in here. He moves her around with him." During the next commercial, Carol lifted the Persian carefully and disappeared with her, probably taking her back to Sam's room. Debra was slightly allergic to cats, and she'd started to sniff.

"Some layout, huh?" I whispered, and Debra rolled her eyes and nodded.

After the soap was over we washed each other's hair. Carol braided mine all over in tiny plaits while it was still wet. Even if we went swimming in the morning, it wouldn't matter, because I just wanted to see how it would look. I wouldn't dare do it on a school night. Debra's hair was naturally curly, so she just combed it and pushed it into shape to dry. Some people get all the good genes.

Just as I'd predicted, I started to get hungry about ten o'clock. Thank goodness for the leftover nachos.

"There's no diet soda." Carol stood looking in her fridge. "Darn Sam. He'll drink anything. I'll bet he's been here all afternoon. He's gone recording crazy since Dad got him a VCR for his birthday. With cable out here there are so many things to watch. He tapes in his room, my room when he can sneak in, and probably Hannah's too. He has enough shows put away to last day and night for a month."

"Put a burglar alarm on your door," I suggested.

"I may have to." Carol finished looking in her refrigerator for diet Dr. Pepper, her favorite soda. "None." She looked as desperate as I had felt the other night when I thought we had no food.

"Listen, let's get the extra nachos, sneak into the kitchen, put them in the microwave, and restock on soda. We won't have to mess up even one pan or dish." I put on my robe.

Carol hesitated, obviously considering it.

"Come on. What harm can it do?" I couldn't imagine being afraid to go into my own kitchen at night, never smelling brownies baking . . . Debra looked at me kind of funny and shrugged her shoulders. I knew she was thinking the same thing.

"Okay," Carol decided, "but stay quiet, you two. I really should go alone. We can't disturb my parents or their guests." Carol led the way so we wouldn't get lost and starve to death in some dark corner of the Barton mansion before a search party found us.

Debra had said "wow" about twenty-five times since we'd gotten off the bus. Now she started it again, but all the time whispering. "Wow, look at this kitchen. What is this, the Barton Hilton?"

I giggled, but I was glad Carol hadn't heard.

We didn't want to give her *too* hard a time. She might never invite us again.

"Look." I pointed. "Hannah's gone to sleep in the line of duty."

Hannah, dressed in her black uniform and frilly white apron, was slumped in her rocker with her shoes off. A headset was fastened atop her gray curls, and a Walkman rested in her lap. On the table beside her was a half-empty glass of that amber liquid they served after dinner every night.

Debra tiptoed over and picked up the glass, sniffing it. She wrinkled her nose and said, "Sherry. Sometimes my mother uses it to help her get to sleep. She says."

"That's funny." Carol got paper plates out of a cupboard for the chips and slipped them out of the foil doggie bag. "Why's Hannah in here so late? I thought dinner would be over by now."

"Should I wake her up and tell her to go to bed?" I giggled, thinking how startled she'd be.

"No. Just look in the pantry for some Peppers." Carol pointed to a door beside the back entrance.

Debra and I tiptoed over. The walk-in pantry was as big as my bedroom and looked like a mini-grocery store.

"Wow! It's your own personal 7-11 convenience store." Debra was in total awe of everything in Carol's house, just as I knew she'd be. As we came out with a six-pack of diet Dr. Pepper in hand she pointed to the box with buttons all over it beside the back door. "What's this?"

"The burglar alarm," I whispered. "Can you imagine? It's a new one, all in some secret code. You have to push a bunch of buttons when you leave and again when you come in." My finger itched to tap a tune on all the tiny buttons while I imagined being the perfect cat burglar. I'd know the combination played "Yankee Doodle" to shut it off, since that's what Mr. Barton had played every time he made a speech while running for office. Then I could steal the million-two in diamonds hidden behind the original Van Gogh in the parlor. I'd take the painting too, if it wasn't too heavy, just because I liked it.

I will never be sure of exactly what happened next, no matter how many times I go over it in my mind. But while we were looking at the alarm system, the buzzer that summons Hannah or Nadia resounded with a loud *ZZZZZ*. I think then that Debra jumped in surprise and pushed me into the black box. Next thing I knew the kitchen was filled with the sound that a dying dinosaur might make. *Augh-augh-augh-augh* magnified twenty times over.

"Maggie!" Carol screamed. "What did you do?"

"I don't know," I shouted back, so I could be heard over the squawking alarm. "But I think I just flunked Spying 303."

I started to shake all over. Debra had a death grip on my right arm. Then I gathered my wits about me long enough to pry her fingers loose and push her into the pantry. At least if we ended up grounded for two weeks, she wouldn't starve. Carol's never been grounded, I reminded myself. What *do* they do to punish criminals at the Barton Hilton? I had this awful feeling that I was about to find out.

"We've got to turn it off." Carol grabbed my arm and pointed me toward the black box. I guess because I turned it on, she thought I'd be able to turn it off.

Even Hannah couldn't sleep through the death throes of a dinosaur. Before she could help us, though, the kitchen door was flung open. Carol turned, grabbed my arm, and both of us stood frozen to the designer vinyl floor.

# *Chapter 7*

Two overdressed people burst into the kitchen, followed by two more.

"Carol, what is going on here?" Mr. Barton shouted.

Of course, Carol had no answer for that question, and the situation was rather straightforward. We'd been caught red-handed raiding the kitchen. Carol still held a foil bag of chips in one hand, and the other hand that was clutching my arm also had three paper plates wadded up in it. Later I wondered if my saying, "Testing, testing, one-two-three," would have saved the day. But there are times when even a sense of humor fails you. I was pretty sure the Bartons didn't think this latest event in the life of their daughter was funny.

But the man behind Mr. Barton, who was also dressed in a tux, did. "Looks like the kitchen is full of desperate criminals, Hubert." He was smoking a cigar, and he leaned on the counter to enjoy what was going to happen next.

I found my voice. "I'm sorry. I think I set off the burglar alarm. It was an accident." I had to shout my apology as the alarm still wailed, *Augh-augh-augh.*

Mr. Barton marched across the room and

shut it off. But by then the police had also arrived. It hadn't taken them much longer than the Bartons to get there. As two uniformed police officers entered the back door, one uniformed maid slipped through the kitchen door that led to the servants' rooms. Hannah had let the police in, but then she melted away like ice in July.

"What's going on here, Mr. Barton?" one officer asked. He had his gun drawn, but he put it away when he saw Carol and me. I guess we looked harmless enough. I thought of my hair and all those wild little braids. Maybe I could pretend I was deranged. My brain raced feverishly: what else? Sleepwalking was out since there were three of us—well, actually two that they could see. I just hoped that Debra kept herself hidden.

By the time the back door opened to reveal Charles and two more policemen, I had recovered my wits enough to understand all the recent media criticism about so much of the budget going for defense. I wondered if *my* neighborhood was so well protected.

"Carol, how could you?" Mrs. Barton moved toward Carol. "This is utterly ridiculous and embarrassing."

"Carol didn't do it, Mrs. Barton. I did." I wasn't one to let my best friend take the blame for my clumsiness.

"Carol is responsible for you," Mrs. Barton said without even looking at me. Ice practically coated her face and dripped from the finger pointed at Carol. Her dress added to the effect.

It was ice blue, draped artfully around her shoulders, her waist, and then falling to the floor. It was more like a blanket of snow or icicles. Or a walking iceberg looking for a *Titanic* to smash into. Carol was no *Titanic*. She was more like a rubber raft deflating under her mother's piercing gaze.

When a policeman came back into the kitchen escorting Debra, I felt like sinking too. "Do you know this young woman? It appears she was hiding in the pantry." How many years can you get for pantry pilfering?

"Carol?" The fluorescent lights of the kitchen danced off the diamonds of Mrs. Barton's throat like the Northern lights.

"I can explain, Mother." Carol summoned a little backbone. As she stepped away from me, I slipped the foil bag from her hand. With the jig up, I wanted to be the one left holding the goods. "This is my friend, Debra Dennison. Debra, I'd like you to meet my mother." Somehow introductions seemed out of place in the script at that point, but maybe Carol knew what she was doing.

Mrs. Barton gave a great sigh, never even acknowledging that Debra existed, turned, and shepherded her guests back to the living-room areas at the far end of the house. Mr. Barton had to stay longer and assure the policemen that there were no desperate criminals in the house and that he didn't intend to press charges against any of us—at the present time, anyway. Perhaps after he counted the soda cans and the paper plates, he'd change his mind.

We forgot about the nachos and soda and went to bed hungry. Or at least I did. I hardly ever lose my appetite. Even under the threat of life imprisonment, I regretted that our mission had gone unaccomplished.

But after I lay there in the dark for about a half hour, knowing no one else would be sleeping either, I remembered that I had brought the foil bag with me when I left the kitchen. None of the policemen had bothered to frisk us.

Somewhere in this room sat a wrinkled but intact doggie bag. I slipped from under the covers and, having an excellent nose for cheese, located the bag easily. Back in bed I hoped the crackle of the foil being opened would go unnoticed, but soon the bed beside me began to shake.

Debra stifled her laughter, sat up, and pulled out of the bag a piece of the cold, but nourishing, emergency rations. In a minute a flashlight nailed us. Carol peeked over the side of the bed, sleeping bag draped over her shoulders.

"You two! At least give me some."

All of us dissolved into carefully concealed laughter. Then while we munched I asked Carol something I was wondering about. "Will your mother really care about Debra being here, Carol?"

"No, it's just that she doesn't like not knowing. She hates surprises."

"I gathered." And our caper had gone way beyond surprises.

Dipping into the bag like starving refugees,

we swiftly destroyed the evidence and, tummies satisfied, we were able to sleep.

The next morning we woke up practically at dawn, of course, having been forced to retire at such an early hour. "If you two will promise me you'll stay right here, I'll go test the temperature of the household." Carol put on her robe and, first looking both ways, disappeared into the hall.

"Think she'll ever return, or will she be thrown into the dungeon for our crimes?" Debra speculated on Carol's punishment.

"I don't think she's ever been grounded." I was glad to stay in bed, hidden in Carol's room. In fact, I wondered if I could manage to stay there for the rest of the week—just to keep out of Mrs. Barton's way.

But obviously we couldn't conceal ourselves from everyone. Our first visitor was Sam. "Hey, Maggie. Is it true that the police came here last night?"

"Yes they did, Sam," I said with a straight face. "Apparently your parents threw such a wild party that the neighbors complained. Someone called the police because they were disturbing the peace."

"Really?" Sam grinned impishly. He loved the idea of that. "Shoot, and I slept through it all. I knew I should have stayed up to watch Johnny Carson. Then I would have still been awake."

This kid had no censorship of his TV viewing at all. Should I bring a countersuit against Mrs. Barton for contributing to the delinquency of a minor? It might be worth a try, but I'd let her make the first move. No use showing my hand until I saw her cards.

But apparently Sam had gotten the straight story before he visited us. "My mom is probably going to kill you." He laughed. "I always miss everything," he complained as he left.

"Maggie doesn't miss anything." Debra leaned back and put both hands behind her head. "I'm not sure you're a good influence on me during my growing-up years."

"Look, you pushed me. I distinctly remember that, now that I think back."

"I got spooked by that buzzer. A trailer does not come equipped with an intercom system, you know. Carol's been gone a long time. Think she'll ever come back?"

"I have no idea. I may get deported. Can I stay at your house the rest of the week?"

"Can you handle returning to the low life with the rest of your friends?"

"It's better than batching with Gerard." Suddenly we heard three kicks on the door. I got up to answer it. Sam never knocked, so I knew it couldn't be him. "What's the secret password?" I called through a thin crack.

"Food." Carol knew the secret word. I let her in and even cleared a place on her desk for the tray she was carrying.

"All's quiet on the western front," she announced, "but Hannah sends a tray and thanks us for covering for her."

"We didn't cover for her, but I guess we did detract attention from her being asleep on the job. Do you think your parents stayed up late enough to sleep through till Friday?" I asked. I could always hope for the best.

"What'll they do?" Debra peeked under the towel spread over the tray. "Hey, French toast and strawberries. All we have is Cheerios on Saturday."

"I really don't know," said Carol in answer to Debra's question about punishment.

"Don't you ever misbehave?" Debra drowned her cinnamon-dusted triangles of toast in maple syrup.

"You can't break rules you don't have." Even while I said that, I knew there were rules at Carol's house. Unwritten ones from her father like: *Stay out from underfoot. See but don't be seen. Don't do anything to embarrass me—your mother—or the family.* The credit card, all the clothes—were they bribes to encourage Carol to be as inconspicuous as possible? To leave her parents to their own lives so they didn't have to bother with children?

I'd think about that more after I'd gotten my share of breakfast. Even with my weird metabolism I just might get fat with someone around to cook for me all the time. Sometimes Mom was too busy to cook and I had to sub. So far, I had mastered baked potatoes, pot pies, and spaghetti. Dad could do goulash and steaks on the charcoal grill. Sometimes we'd both give up and go get Chinese takeout food. It was fun going out with Dad when he was hungry because he'd buy one of everything. Hey, what was I doing thinking about my parents? Just shows you what one narrow escape can do to screw up your thinking.

We polished off Hannah's breakfast, looked up the clothing sales in three newspapers, then got dressed and slipped outside to the pool. Might as well enjoy our freedom while it lasted.

Just lying around could get in my blood, I realized after an hour in the sun with only a few laps thrown in to assuage my guilt. Then Sam appeared with snorkle, swim fins, and an armful of snacks. "Hannah says you have to watch me."

"Okay." Carol sat up and slathered herself with oil again. "Holler if you're drowning."

Sam had probably been swimming since he was two. I did watch him for a few minutes, and he swam like an Olympic tot, diving to pull dead leaves from the bottom of the pool.

Debra had afternoon classes to teach, so she got dressed at the pool house. I thought she was chicken to leave before we found out the repercussions of the night before, but she said she'd return for sentencing if necessary.

Carol had relieved our minds somewhat. "Hannah said she eavesdropped after things calmed down last night. Mr. Stetwiler, the guy who came in the kitchen with my parents, had a big laugh over the whole thing. So maybe Daddy won't be too mad if we didn't upset his plans. He was trying to get Stetwiler's endorsement for his campaign."

Mr. Barton found us eating lunch in the kitchen. We got a polite lecture on carelessness, and then he showed Carol how the new system worked. I said "Yes, sir," a couple of times, but otherwise kept quiet. So did Carol. It seemed as if Carol tried to ignore her parents as much as they ignored her. There was sort of a formal side-by-side existence here: if you don't get in our way, we won't get in yours. Was Carol happy to take all the bribes and conform, or had she just gotten used to it? One of the skills of being a kid is learning to live with the system. It struck me as funny that I hadn't learned as fast or as well as Carol. While I wasn't about to run away from home or anything that drastic, I did find I had to speak my mind or protest occasionally.

"Let's go to the afternoon movie," Carol suggested when we got back to her room. She was picking up any evidence of last night's eating or sleeping.

I was used to jobs at home, but all Carol was responsible for was her room, and that only to keep anyone else out. I agreed to the plan and pulled on some old jeans. I'd save my new ones for school. Carol had a favorite pair that were faded by wear, not fashion. She offered to lend me a sweater, and I was in the closet choosing when I heard her talking to someone. I realized it was her mother, so I stayed in the closet.

"Your guest may stay through the week, Carol, since her parents are gone and we did make an agreement, but you may not have company again until you've thought a long time about that perfectly ridiculous scene in the kitchen last night. Is that clear?"

"Yes, Mother."

"What are your plans for the afternoon?" Did Mrs. Barton really care or did she want to make sure Carol didn't ride her bike into a tea party or something?

"We're going to a movie, Mother, then we're going to do a little shopping."

"I certainly hope you aren't going to wear those old jeans to town."

"Yes, I was. They're fine, Mother. Everyone wears them. Even the new ones—you buy them already faded."

"What will people think? That we can't afford to keep our only daughter in decent clothing? Your friend can dress any way she pleases, but you have a reputation to uphold. With your father running for public office—"

"All right, all right, Mother. I'll change." That was the closest I ever heard Carol come to disagreeing with her mother. But in the end she gave up easily.

Carol came into the closet. I whispered, "Is she gone?"

"Yeah." Carol jerked off her jeans, threw them on a hook, and started pawing through her skirts. Pulling a green plaid one from a hanger, she tugged it on. Then she had to put on panty hose, of course, and a nice pair of loafers instead of tennis shoes.

I watched in sympathy, realizing I'd never seen Carol at school in jeans. I found myself feeling glad I had no reputation to maintain. Well, no parents' reputation to maintain, that is.

As for myself, I could choose. Even if I wanted to be a nerd, my parents probably wouldn't interfere. If I chose to be a brain, on the other hand, they'd positively rejoice.

But it was *my* choice.

# Chapter 8

We got through the rest of the weekend without any mishaps, and I found myself almost looking forward to going to school Monday morning. I was sure now that Mrs. Barton didn't like me, and I just couldn't get used to having every dinnertime turn into a tense situation. Saturday and Sunday nights' dinners proved to be every bit as rigid and formal as had my first meal there.

I adopted Carol's attitude of "you ignore me, I'll ignore you." We stayed in her room when we were home and concentrated on clothes, homework, and thinking about the possibility of Dobs or Rob ever asking us for a date.

Rob had stopped me in the hall twice more to talk, but still no date, not even for help with math. Once before algebra class when he asked about the homework assignment, I had the feeling that he was just using math as an excuse to talk to me. But math was all he did talk about.

Another time he stopped at my locker when Dobs was talking to Carol. I wanted so much to have it mean something, but I was afraid to get my hopes up. How long does a guy have to go on making small talk before he commits himself to a date? Even a study date? I felt pretty confident that he liked me, though, so I was determined to be patient. Besides, I never saw him with any other girl in the hall, and that was also a good sign.

The same pattern of Charles driving us and our getting off at the corner continued. I couldn't persuade Carol to indulge in the luxury of door-to-door service. I had to admit that I loved the notion of all of Hammond High watching *me* getting out of a Mercedes. Magnolia Howell, poor little rich girl, condescends to attend public high school with the peons.

By Wednesday Carol noticed that I'd been wearing my new jeans for three days in a row.

"Hey, Maggie, there's no one here to tell you how to dress. Tomorrow you're going to school as the new Maggie Howell."

"But I was just beginning to get comfortable with the old one," I protested as we poked through the rows of Carol's skirts and blouses.

"First of all, a dress. Well, no, you can't wear my dresses, they'd be too short. But I'll bet we can find a skirt and blouse that would fit you."

"Not that one that puts me in mourning. Black definitely does nothing for me." I found Carol's enthusiasm contagious, and she was right. I'd better take the risk of entering the world of high fashion while I still could. As soon as my parents returned, I'd go back to being Miss Average Plain Jane USA.

"How about this? I've never even worn it." Carol pulled out a soft green skirt that just escaped being preppy because the seams were on the outside, making it look wrong-side-out.

It was a big style at school for the kids who wore stuff other than jeans. Sort of like wearing a sweat shirt inside-out.

I stopped trying to imagine what it would be like to actually have an outfit in my closet that I'd never even worn and pulled my red Pep Club sweater over my head. Both Felicity and Maud, the antique Persian, sat on Carol's bed, watching the transformation of Maggie Howell, Miss Average in All Ways, to Magnolia Howell, teen model, about to be photographed in her what-to-wear-to-algebra look. Algebra reminded me of Rob Tyler, and that made me even more enthusiastic. A new look might be just the thing to bring him around.

The sweater that matched the skirt, which was one shade lighter, was soft and fuzzy. I only hoped some poor little rabbit hadn't had to die so I could wear it. I'd wear furs that got shed, but not furs that had to leave an animal shivering.

Felicity sniffed my back suspiciously as I sat on the bed to turn the tops of a pair of green socks down as far over my Nikes as I could. Carol wore a size-six shoe, and I wore eight, so there was no hope of borrowing more stylish footwear. I had black flats and one pair of panty hose, so I'd probably go for those tomorrow when this makeover would be for real.

Someone knocked at the door. Maud had already given me a withering look reminiscent of Mrs. Barton's, so I hoped this wasn't madame in the flesh. I could imagine her saying to Carol that she simply couldn't afford to outfit all of Carol's friends.

"Who is it?" Carol asked, glancing around her room. Was she checking the state of the room's cleanliness while we occupied it?

Sam came in. "It's me, Carol. Can I have a soda? Mother and Father are having an argument in the kitchen, and I think I'd better stay up here." Didn't Sam have his own refrigerator?

"What are they fighting about?" Carol took a Pepsi out of her fridge and handed it to Sam. She had made sure it was always full after our brush with the law.

"Whether or not Mom can go to her bridge club or whether she has to go to a tea some lady is having for the candidates." Sam sat in Carol's rocker to watch us, but Carol marched over to her door and pointed for him to leave.

I felt relieved Mr. and Mrs. Barton were fighting over something important rather than whether or not to send me home. But as I watched Sam get up reluctantly, I felt a twinge of sympathy for him. He was lonely. Where were his neighborhood pals, his friends from school? Didn't he ever have any company, either? What Sam really needed was Gerard, and I made a mental note to have Carol bring him to my house with her someday. Gerard would get a good workout with an energetic five-year-old. He needed it. He was getting fat.

Carol turned her attention back to me. First she took the curling iron and styled my hair so that it swept away from my face instead of into it. Next she set out a tray of cosmetics, like a painter's palette, and began to instruct me as to their uses. A painted lady. I smiled. I had some vague, useless, tucked-away information in my head from somewhere: a butterfly. Was I about to become a butterfly instead of a caterpillar?

She shadowed my eyes with light green and penciled lines above and below to widen them. At first I thought I looked like a surprised punk-rock star. Then Carol realized it was too much all at once and toned down the whole effect. I argued that I had on too much foundation too, but she said it took a lot to cover my freckles.

"*Voilà,*" she said at last. "Rob Tyler will fall right out of his chair when he sees you."

"I'm glad! Maybe the football coach will give me a medal for keeping him awake in algebra class long enough to pass."

"Maybe you should pin him down about helping him with his work, the way you help me. He's given you the opening. Be a little bit aggressive." Carol handed me the color lipstick she had chosen for a finishing effect.

"You mean you think we should actually work on math problems for an hour?" I had to think Carol's fantasy life wasn't too rich. If I was going to daydream about spending time with Rob Tyler, I could come up with something a lot better than working on algebra problems.

"After a study session, you'd need to go get a hamburger to get back the strength you'd used up thinking. One thing would lead to another."

"True. We would be the lucky couple eating the hundred billionth hamburger at McDonald's, and we'd win a trip for two to Hawaii. Then a hurricane would strand us in a little cabin at the bottom of a dead volcano where we had gone to find fossils from the Mesozoic era."

"Maggie, I don't know why you don't write one of those novels your mother is always typing. Your fantasies are wilder than any plot I've ever read."

Mention of my mom took part of the fun out of putting on the earrings Carol had handed me, the same ones I'd coveted in the shopping mall. How could I be feeling homesick when I looked so alluring?

After three turns in front of the mirror on the back of Carol's bathroom door, I gave up and looked at my watch. It was after five. I'd better call Mom and see what was going on. I wondered why they hadn't called me by now. Had they forgotten they had a lovely, charming daughter who might grow up on them if they didn't hurry back to keep her frozen in time? Or had they gotten off by themselves, remembered how much fun it was not to have any responsibilities, and decided children were to be born and ignored as best they could—like some people whose name I won't mention?

"Maggie, sweet baby," Mom answered the phone. "I was just thinking of calling. Are you surviving?" Mom sounded so good that I didn't even mind her calling me "baby," so I guessed that Aunt Ruth was getting better too. Mom confirmed it and said they'd like to stay until Sunday if it was okay with me and Carol. I asked Carol and she said sure. She wouldn't be able to invite me back for a while, so we'd better stretch this visit out as long as possible. I talked to Mom for a minute longer, then Dad, then I said hi to Aunt Ruth and Uncle Roger. It was a nice touching-base conversation, and I felt kind of all warm inside after we hung up.

Carol had left the room while I finished talking, and now she was back with an idea. "Mother and Father left, and I persuaded Nadia to make spaghetti. Let's call Debra and have her meet us at the Video Connection after dinner. We'll have Charles drive us down, get a flick, and come back here and watch it. Then he can drive her home. Daddy took his own car."

I looked at Carol in total surprise. "Are you sure you want to do that?" We hadn't had any more run-ins with the security system or the police and were playing it pretty safe. We'd made sure to stock up on ice cream and snacks so once we got home from school we could stay up in Carol's room. What Carol was suggesting now was close to total rebellion.

"I can't get in much more trouble." Carol smiled.

"You are getting mighty close to misbehaving there, young lady," I said as sternly as possible.

"You're a bad influence on me, Maggie." Carol laughed. "Thank goodness."

We had a great time. We got two old James Dean movies and smuggled Debra in, knowing that neither Charles nor Hannah would rat on us. We popped popcorn, but Carol made me do it in the closet, saying she didn't want oil on her carpet. I shrugged, figuring she couldn't switch over to being both a sneak and a slob in one evening.

Debra decided that Jamie Patterson looked a lot like James Dean and figured he'd probably give up chewing tobacco if he really liked a girl. She said she was going to give him another chance.

I could hardly wait till morning to give Rob Tyler another chance too. According to my calculations, we were almost up to casual encounter number forty-two, since I saw him at least once a day, and he'd spoken to me a lot since the swimming party. But I wasn't one to try to rush a guy. I realized most of them are shy and want to be sure a girl won't say no if they ask for a date. Just getting that great smile of his directed at me was enough to keep me going for a long time.

"How early do we have to get up to create this transformation in the morning?" I asked after Debra had gone home. I couldn't quite get used to my new image, no matter how long I spent staring into the mirror. I looked at least twenty years old. I hoped I wouldn't look too mature and sophisticated to Rob. That is, unless he had always wished he could meet an older woman. In that case, I'd be about right.

"Count on about half an hour extra," Carol answered my question. "Take a shower and wash your hair tonight. We can leave all this junk out if we clean up in the morning." Carol put away the cosmetics we hadn't used. She had about three of every tube and bottle and plastic case.

\*     \*     \*

I'll admit I felt pretty nervous the next morning. It had taken so long to fix me up that we only had time to grab bananas and a glass of milk for breakfast as we ran through the kitchen and out the back door. I wished I had a granola bar, but I knew Charles would never let us eat in the Mercedes anyway. I'd probably faint from hunger by the end of the second period, and that would get me even more attention than my new look.

It would make the headlines of the *Hammond Review*. DYING BEAUTY SUCCUMBS TO LOW BLOOD SUGAR. "Miss Magnolia Howell, star Pep Club member, passed away in the arms of football star Rob Tyler today. Her dying words as she brushed her auburn curls away from the earrings dangling from her lovely earlobes were, 'A chocolate bar would have saved the day.' Unfortunately none of the algebra class carried emergency rations. Rob Tyler is disconsolate. Her cheers will be missed in the bleachers of Hammond High."

Suddenly I realized that the car wasn't moving anymore. "Maggie, are you going to get out of the car," Carol said, shaking me by the shoulder. "Charles says my mother needs the car back at the house right away. She has an early beauty-shop appointment." Carol peered in at me, still dreamily lounging on the leather seat covers.

I climbed out gracefully, catching a glimpse of myself in the rearview mirror and feeling thankful that my auburn tints were natural—except, perhaps, if I had a good secretary, I could dictate my novel while a beauty parlor stylist prepared me to meet my public.

"Maggie, stop that daydreaming. You are consciously trying to escape real life; and today, at least, you should stick around and see how many real men fall in love with you." Carol had no patience at all with my fantasies.

"Oh, yes, I'd almost forgotten about the new me. *Femme fatale* of Hammond High. Pass by all the men and let them weep." I strolled up the hill.

Carol shook her head while we opened up our lockers. "You've got to take yourself more seriously, Maggie. Men may laugh at funny women, but do they date them?"

I took a deep breath and tried to get more in the spirit of the new me. But first chance I got, I was going to write a letter to Carol Burnett. "Dear Carol. Did you have many dates in high school or did it take a mature man to see through to the real you and appreciate your sense of humor? Write right back. I may have to change my personality in a hurry." I might even mail it special delivery.

Harold Tubbs started laughing when I got to biology class, and I hadn't even said anything. "Is that you, Maggie? What have you done to yourself?"

"I have grown up, Harold. And until you do, I'd appreciate it if you wouldn't speak to me again." I didn't wait for him to say anything else. There are times when one has to stop being nice to everyone, and Harold's time had come. I knew about all the statistics showing that girls matured faster than boys, and Harold was a prime example. He was going to stay a pudgy ten-year-old for another three years, at least.

I got through a pop quiz, a day early, in biology, and finding out that I knew all about protozoa gave me just that much more confidence in myself. By the time I strolled into algebra, I was Brooke Shields, pursuing an education along with the admiration of *thinking* men. Looks, personality, intelligence—I had them all.

Rob couldn't take his eyes off me, and I almost forgot my gnawing hunger until my stomach rumbled loud enough to register five-point-five on the Richter scale. I lowered my eyes, whispered "hush," and looked around to see if anyone had noticed.

One of the breath mints I had been hoarding might appease my tummy, as well as prepare me for talking to Rob—if he could get over being speechless—at the end of class. I dug in my purse, brushed the lint off the little white disk, and popped it into my mouth. Then I got out my calculator and pretended I didn't know men existed.

Being poised meant I couldn't run to catch up with Rob after class, so I had to settle for a smile as he looked back before he disappeared into the mass of humanity that poured through the halls at Hammond for each class change.

I suited up for PE and hoped we wouldn't have to do anything that made me sweat too much. I forgot to check if the new mascara Carol opened for me was waterproof. I didn't want streaks in the foundation either. It was rather satisfying to feel the sexy earrings bounce against my cheeks as we jumped around trying to get a volleyball over the net.

"Well, Debra. How do you like the new me?" I asked as we changed back to street clothes.

"Your mom would have a fit," Debra said as she tied her suede saddle shoes.

"I didn't ask you to be my mother. I know I can't get by with this look when I return home, but let's call it a preview of the future—when I have control of my own life." I checked my face closely and refreshed my mascara quickly before we had to go to lunch.

"I think I'll wait till all the votes are in." Debra refused to express an opinion. It wasn't like her.

I took one last look, trying to see me as she did. I did look different, but . . . I thought I liked it. Didn't I?

In the cafeteria we met Carol and went to the grill together. Buying my lunch instead of lugging it from home in a paper bag all week had been fun. Today I ordered a burger and fries and a milkshake, then picked up a carton of yogurt and an apple for later. I don't know how I had had the energy to get through PE.

"We didn't have time for breakfast." I felt I had to explain the presence of so much food to Debra, even though she was perfectly familiar with my constant need for nourishment.

"I noticed." She had a chicken salad with no bread and tea with no sugar. "But my leotard would bulge in all the wrong places if I ate like you do all the time. I know I dance off a lot of calories, but I have to be realistic too."

"Look, Maggie," Carol whispered, pretending to reach for the salt. "Rob Tyler can't take his eyes off you." I don't know why Carol had to whisper. Rob and Jamie and Dobs were two tables away. But sure enough, when I peeked, Rob was looking in my direction. My heart skipped a beat, and I had trouble swallowing. I even had to leave two bites of bun on my plate, I got so wiggly inside.

"Cute earrings, Maggie," Mary Fern Davidson said to me as she got up from the table behind us. "You look nice today."

"Thanks, Mary Fern," I managed to say. Carol smiled at me, and I felt glad to have such a good friend, who would help me look my best, bring out my best qualities, and understand what was right for me.

The three of us had English together after lunch, and then I set off for typing alone. Rob was in that class too, and I felt really lucky to share two subjects with him since he was a junior. He smiled again before class started, and then I proceeded to make nine mistakes in my business letter to Generic College Number One, in which I was supposed to ask for campus work and an application for a student scholarship. I wondered if Rob was going to college, and if so, where? It would be funny if we ended up together at Colorado State. I was going there if I couldn't get in the university. He'd remember me from high school and say he was glad I'd come to his school. He had been lonely for a whole year. I would say he should have written me, and he would say he was too busy writing business letters to prospective employers and the Peace Corps.

He'd suggest I join the Peace Corps too, and we'd find ourselves assigned to battle ignorance together in the heart of Zambuie's steaming jungles. Two years of satisfying work together would make us realize we made an inseparable team, one that should stay together forever.

I found I'd signed my letter "Yours Forever," instead of "Sincerely," so I had to white out twelve more letters. It was the worst paper I'd typed all year. I'd definitely have to have a secretary for my novel.

By the time class was over, I wasn't surprised to find Rob waiting for me. If we were going to be a team, we'd need to get started as soon as possible.

"Hi, Maggie," he said, falling in step beside me as I moved slowly toward French class.

"Oh, hello, Rob. Ready for tomorrow's game?" It was safer to talk about football than to start right off discussing the Peace Corps. And maybe football would lead to talking about other sports, such as going to the movies and parking.

"Maggie . . ." Rob hesitated as if he didn't know how to put what he was going to say next. I guess I'd never thought about how hard it was for a guy to ask a girl for a date the first time. "I'd like to think we are . . . friends."

Oh, yes, I know we are, I said silently. I didn't know what to say out loud. Finally I squeezed out the word "yes" and nodded at the same time in case it stuck in my throat. Also I wanted to set the earrings in motion.

"Friends should be honest with each other, don't you think?"

I nodded again, wondering if I could handle his telling me right off that he had loved me from the minute he set eyes on me.

He stopped and I almost bumped into him. Quickly I stepped back, since I found myself standing much too close to him. He had beautiful blue eyes, and his blue sweater made them an even deeper shade.

Whatever he had to say must be really hard for him, and I wanted to help him. I wanted to say, "I love you too, Rob. It's okay. I know we're young, but say it. We'll work it out." But before I could decide on anything to say, he blurted out, "All that makeup is wrong for you, Maggie. It makes you look funny. And I kinda liked your freckles."

Then he hurried off before I could say anything—something nasty like I would have to Harold Tubbs—anything funny to cover my hurt feelings. Trouble was, when I was around Harold I always had a bunch of remarks ready. I hadn't had any ready for Rob. He had totally caught me by surprise.

All this time I'd thought he was having a hard time asking me for a date or telling me how much he was in love with me. And all he'd stopped me for was to tell me I looked funny.

# Chapter 9

I made it to the bathroom before I started to cry. Then I hid in a stall until the second bell rang and I had recovered a little. When I finally came out, I walked right over to the mirror.

Ignoring my red eyes, I made an honest appraisal. The conclusion I finally came to was something I guess I'd known all along. I did look funny. Well, not funny, exactly, but not me. I had let Carol convince me I looked glamorous and grown up, but I didn't really. I looked like fifteen-year-old Maggie Howell with a pound and a half of expensive cosmetics layered on my face.

Maybe Carol had practiced longer on herself. She looked all right with makeup on. She looked like the person I'd met and made friends with this year. It was *her*. But it wasn't me—at all. Where a touch of mascara and some lip gloss enhanced my looks, all this goo covered up, hid what I really looked like. Was that what I wanted? To hide what I looked like? My freckles were disguised. Where are my freckles? The real me?

It took me ten minutes to remember the rest of what Rob had said. "I kinda liked your freckles."

I grabbed the bar of soap on the lavatory

sink, forgetting the fact that it had been used by dozens of dirty hands, and ran warm water to make a lather. When the rinse water stopped running peach, I was satisfied that the makeup was all gone. The new Maggie Howell had gone down the drain. The old one was back. I dug in my purse, found some lotion, and rubbed it on my face so my skin wouldn't be so dry. Then I took out my mascara and lightly touched my lashes. Same with the cherry lip gloss.

There she is, Miss Freckle Face. I tried to smile. I have a two-thousand-dollar smile, my dad says. If I have to look funny, though, I'll look naturally funny, not disguised funny. The tears started down my cheeks again. How could he! How could Rob just out and out tell me I looked funny? He could at least have hinted. I'd have gotten the message since I had some doubts about the new look myself. I knew he didn't mean to be cruel. He meant well. He likes my freckles, I reminded myself.

Will the real Maggie Howell stand up? I made a face at the mirror. "I like your freckles," I said aloud. "I do too," Rob Tyler echoed from somewhere behind me. If only he'd keep telling me that . . .

I wrinkled my nose, making the brown spots run together. The face with the dancing freckles. Men were charmed by her dancing freckles. I tried out the line. Not your basic romance, but maybe it would work if the main character had a super personality. She could have a great sense of humor, be a good listener, and demonstrate empathy for the masses.

Finally I stopped looking in the mirror, which helped. I took five deep breaths and swallowed the lump in my throat. I would live through this. I might never look at Rob again, but I would survive. I am a survivor, I reminded myself. Every horoscope I read says I am a survivor. Surely, in time, I will remember other, worse things that have happened.

By the time I had regained my poise and had the guts to leave the bathroom, French period was half over. I knew I couldn't go in this late. If I could get past a hall monitor, I'd report into the office tomorrow morning for an absence slip for Miss Peters.

I'd say I got sick and had to go home early. I'd say I spent half the period in the bathroom throwing up and didn't want to expose the whole French class to my germs. I'd tell them my mother was out of town on an emergency and they'd just have to believe me. With my innocent and charming face, I was sure I could pull it off.

Looking both ways, I hurried to the front door. I hated to take all my afternoon class books home, but at least I had a ride. I'd borrow Carol's algebra book and since we'd had the biology quiz today, tomorrow would just be a lab or something.

I almost ran down the walk and then downhill toward where Charles parked and met us. I'd have to hope Carol would come right out to the car and not spend time hunting for me.

"Good afternoon, Charles," I said politely. "I hope you had a nice day. I got out early, but Carol will be here in a few minutes."

Charles had been reading a book while he waited for us. Charles usually read mystery novels while he waited, but today he was studying a book whose title blared: *One Way to Write Your Novel*. He only looked up for a second, then nodded, got out, and opened the door for me.

Charmed by her cute, freckled face, men leaped to open doors for her. It was a face that launched a thousand Mercedes.

I sat there a few minutes, thinking. I didn't want to keep thinking, but somehow I couldn't stop. Life's like that. There are days, days like today, when I feel I don't want to keep on living, but somehow I can't stop. I try to remember that if I can hang on, I'll age—like fine wine. Next year I'll be sixteen and get my driver's license, and that should be so much fun for a year before it gets to be a habit, something I'll just end up doing automatically.

Look at Charles, though. He's made a career of driving. I guess I wouldn't like that, unless I could be a race-car driver or something. Somehow I don't think I'm the type of person with the guts to hurtle around a track at two hundred miles an hour, though. So I'll just concentrate on negotiating the streets of Cedarhurst and think of something else to do for a living.

In two years I'll be seventeen and a senior, and that's when I'll really get my life together. Maybe I won't be football queen or president of the class, but there will be some niche for me. If all else fails, I can be a counselor for sophomore girls, giving them pep talks and telling them that being fifteen isn't the end of the world.

I leaned back onto the smooth, cool seat and looked out the window. Then why did I still feel like it was? How could Rob Tyler tell me I looked funny? Harold Tubbs, maybe, but Rob Tyler? Anger started to bubble up from deep inside me.

"Maggie?" Debra's head appeared in the open door.

"What!" I snapped, and then realized who it was.

"Well, don't bite my head off. Where's Carol?"

"I don't know. I cut French."

"You cut French? Miss Peters will kill you. What will you tell her tomorrow? Why'd you cut French?" Debra was justified in asking all those questions. I was one of those people who is afraid to break even the tiniest school rule. For me, cutting a class was on a scale with refusing to pay income tax or not curtsying to the queen of England.

Quickly I made a decision. "Charles, tell Carol I'll be home later and that I'm taking the bus." I slid out of the car onto the sidewalk and motioned for Debra to come with me. We walked for a block in silence and then ran to catch the city bus that stops downtown.

"Aren't you going to Carol's? Are your parents home?" Debra couldn't stop. Sometimes I think she's worse than my mother.

"Keep going. You have fifteen more questions before you get to twenty. I don't mind at all playing Twenty Questions, and I'm sure I can think of a prize worthy of your curiosity." There I was taking my anger out on poor Debra, and she had nothing to do with it. I guess that's the risk of being friends with someone. Displaced anger, I believe it's called. You kick me. I'm afraid to kick you back. So I kick the dog. I should be kicking Rob Tyler. I'm afraid to kick Rob Tyler.

"Meow." Debra smiled to soften her comment. I guess she didn't mind being kicked as long as she could find out why eventually. "Maybe you need some chocolate ice cream, Maggie. Let's go to Steve's. I'll treat."

Steve's was a new ice cream parlor at the downtown Cedarhurst mall. We'd be more likely to encounter Fairview High kids there, but that was fine. At least no one from Hammond would come up to me and say, "Hi, Maggie. Wow, you sure made a fool of yourself at school today." If Debra noticed that I'd washed my face and taken off my earrings, she kept quiet about it. I guess if she really had finished Twenty Questions, she'd have gotten around to it.

We hopped off the bus at Broadway and Walnut and walked the three blocks to Steve's. The weather was still nice enough so that the mall hummed with people. The leaves on the trees were all golden. Some fell onto the red-brick pavement and made a satisfying crunching sound underfoot.

Gone were the jugglers, the mime, the musicians. But the people themselves in Cedarhurst were interesting enough to sit and watch. A number of spectators were doing just that. Others sat at the outdoor tables at the New York Delicatessen or Napolitano's, Cedarhurst's best pizza place in the opinion of some. They were laughing and talking. No one had insulted them. No one had told them that they looked funny.

Three punkers sauntered by. One had yellow hair in a Mohawk, except it didn't stop at his collar but trailed six inches down his back. His girlfriend's hair was dyed maroon and partly crew cut. The other guy looked almost normal except for a streak of white down the middle of his head like a skunk. I guess they went to Fairview High, since I'm sure I would have noticed them at Hammond. Was Fairview High any different than Hammond? Maybe I could transfer there if I got some awful reputation at Hammond.

As we approached Steve's at the upper end of Pearl Street I could see all the way up into the canyon and the foothills. Evergreens mingled with aspen in a green and gold salute to October. Sugarloaf Mountain was softly silhouetted against that azure blue sky that only Colorado seems to have. Maybe I should just start walking into the mountains and hibernate like some old bear. When I woke up in the spring, I'd be much older, and maybe some miracle like the ugly-duckling story would have transpired. I'd be beautiful. People would say, "That's the girl that used to look funny. She's changed somehow, don't you think?"

Rob would remember me, but he'd have to look twice. "I can't believe I once told you you looked funny," he'd say. "Can you ever forgive me?"

"I'll have to think about it," I'd say as I prepared to interview the lineup of men who wanted dates with me.

"We've reached our destination." Debra pushed me through the door into the ice cream parlor.

We ordered sundaes with lots of gooey syrup and whipped cream on the top. I began to feel better just watching the girl pile on nuts for good measure.

"Okay, give." Debra had waited as long as she could stand to. When we got seated, she positively demanded an explanation. "You and Carol have a fight?"

"Oh, no. I hope she doesn't get worried about where I went." Then I poured out the whole story between bites of ice cream and sweet goo.

"Rob Tyler actually had the nerve to say that to you? Tell you you looked funny? I can't believe this. No guy I know except Harold Tubbs would do that." Debra licked her spoon after every bite.

"I can't believe it, either. But he did. I'll never be able to look at him again." Maybe I'd just eat and eat till I get so fat I won't care. How long would that take? Can you die of chocolate sundae overdose? I scooped up another big bite. I'd be willing to try.

"But he did say he likes freckles." Debra scraped the remains of the syrup from her cardboard bowl. "I wish I had freckles. If you decide not to ever speak to him again, let me know. Maybe I can fake them with eyeliner pencil."

I ignored Debra's willingness to take on a leftover suitor so eagerly. "Debra, I just wanted to die. Carol said I looked great. And I thought I looked great. I looked at least five years older. No one ever tells Carol she looks funny with makeup on."

Debra stared out the window for a minute. People strolled in the yellow scudding leaves. Trees on the mall were at their best. The lowering sun shimmering through them made each branch look as if it waved the contents of a treasure chest. Then Debra looked at me and said some things that reminded me of why I sometimes think she's more mature than Carol and me, why she's a treasured friend to me.

"Carol doesn't look funny with makeup on, Maggie. But you aren't Carol. I could never wear as much stuff on my face as she does. First of all, I'd get zits. Secondly, I can't afford all those cosmetics. Third, *I'd* look funny."

I rubbed a sore spot on my chin. A small lump signaled the beginning of a pimple. Was it because I'd clogged my pores all day?

"Maybe Rob did you a favor, Maggie," Debra continued. "I couldn't get up the nerve to tell you I didn't like the way you looked this morning. You didn't really look five years older. You looked like Maggie Howell, pretending to be older. You didn't look like you. It's taken me a long time to realize I have to look like me, Maggie. So do you. We don't have any choice."

Debra wasn't exactly pretty. But then she wasn't

ugly either. She fell sort of into the same category that I did. We both looked okay. Debra has a nice smile now that she got her braces taken off. I have freckles and a ski-jump nose that some people would label cute. Because of it, though, I will never be beautiful. "Maggie, yes, I know her. She's that girl that might be beautiful if her nose didn't turn up at the end." There are no cosmetics or techniques of shadowing that can hide a tilted nose.

I looked at Debra. She turned on her thousand-dollar smile. She hadn't needed as much straightening as I had. "Thanks, Deb. How come you have so much more sense than I do?"

"Well, I am older." Debra was born in March. I was born in September. She *was* older—and wiser. Would six months do that much for me? Like I said before, I know if I can just hold on, I'll survive. I might not even have to hibernate all winter.

"Do you and Carol want to spend the night Friday after the game? You can pretend you're slumming." Debra continued to grin.

"We could rig a burglar alarm with tin cans and a string. When a good-looking cat burglar falls over them, he'll be trapped with three luscious women."

Debra got me laughing again. Mom read that book about the man who laughed himself healthy after being diagnosed as having a fatal disease. Maybe I could laugh myself back to wanting to live after the most humiliating day of my life. Maybe I could laugh myself right past Harold Tubbs, Rob Tyler, and anyone else who doesn't appreciate me and into the arms of a mature man who knows that beauty is only skin deep. He'd know to look into the very soul of any woman he wants. I'm sure I have a very beautiful soul inside me someplace.

People on the mall as we window-shopped back to the bus stop probably thought, Look at those dippy teenage girls. For just a few minutes I was almost glad I was only fifteen and could get away with acting silly in public. Will wonders ever cease?

Rob Tyler has done me a favor? Now if I can only believe that, maybe, just maybe, I'll have the guts to smile at him tomorrow. Show him I have no hard feelings.

My smile will say, "Look here at this beautiful soul that you have saved from wandering down the wrong path of life."

# *Chapter 10*

Carol was a bit miffed because I'd gone off without her, but then her curiosity about why I wasn't in French class got the better of her. She took her anger out on Rob.

"How dare he! Did you slap him? Or at least turn and stomp away?" Carol's hands were on her hips, and she was both telling and showing me what *she* would have done. *She* would *not* have gone in the bathroom and cried and scrubbed off her makeup. We're different, I reminded myself. That kept me from trying to explain about how I'd decided he was right.

We didn't have long to talk, either, since it was dinnertime. I wore the borrowed green outfit to dinner, but when we got back to Carol's room, I slipped out of it, hanging it up carefully, and pulled on my comfortable old jeans. I wore them all the time at home, and no one ever complained. That cute Maggie with her ragged jeans. I fingered the hole that was growing at the knee.

While we were studying, I told Carol about Debra's invitation. "Her mother won't be home," I added. "She and one of her girlfriends are going to a retreat to examine their self-image." Retreat and self-image. Somehow the two words fit nicely together. I went back to thinking about running away for a couple of years. I could live in the mountains and eat roots and berries. The natural vitamins would be good for my complexion.

The next morning I pulled on my red Pep Club sweater and my new jeans. If Mom and Dad didn't get back soon, I'd have to put them in the stack of clothes that Carol put outside her door every morning. Then in the afternoon they'd return magically clean. Somewhere in the depths of the Barton mansion a washing machine spun away quietly. But Carol never loaded it. I wondered if she had ever missed the sweet smell of freshly washed clothes from the clothesline. No, I guess you don't miss something you've never been exposed to.

We managed to jam all our stuff into one overnight bag, asked Charles not to pick us up after school, and told Hannah where we'd be. She never even questioned Carol's spending the night somewhere else. Carol hadn't asked her mother. Didn't her mother care where she was? It seemed all Carol had to do for permission was *tell* Hannah. Secretly I had to laugh at my mom thinking I was well supervised because I was at Carol's.

"Oh, Hannah," I imagined us saying. "Carol and I are taking off for California for a few days."

"Fine, Miss Maggie. I'll tell Nadia not to set a place for you tonight. And if you have any dirty clothes, just save them until you get back."

All day long at school I avoided Rob Tyler.

Why was it that all of a sudden I saw him everywhere? We had only the two classes together. But I'd look away or turn around whenever I saw him. Did he wonder what was wrong? Or did he think, I shouldn't have said that to Maggie. Now she's angry at me. I'll have to go down on bended knee to get her to forgive me. Again, although I knew he was right, I couldn't believe he'd actually said what he said to me, and I was too embarrassed to ever look at him again.

It was fun being at Debra's. Everything about the trailer was messy and comfortable. It was within walking distance of the school, and we didn't mind being on foot at all because the glorious autumn days were still lingering on.

In the distance the Boulders, rock formations famous in Cedarhurst, pushed their granite slabs up against the blue sky. Wisps of clouds drifted back and forth across the tips of them. The bases were furred with dark evergreens, which, at this distance, looked sort of like whiskers. It wouldn't be long before they would be dusted with snow. I had tried cross-country skiing in the meadow below last winter. This year I hoped to go on some real trails. Carol couldn't believe I wasn't an accomplished skier, but not everyone in Colorado is. I like having my feet firmly under me, not sliding all around.

Did Rob ski? But I wasn't supposed to be thinking about Rob. I was never going to speak to him again, remember?

By five o'clock there was a hint of winter's

chill in the air, but it made us feel all snuggly in our sweaters.

For supper, we grilled ham-and-cheese sandwiches, chopped coleslaw, and devoured the last of a carrot cake Deb's mom had made the first of the week. Since Mrs. Dennison had classes afternoons and nights, she slept late and was around the house all day. She believed in eating well. She and Debra didn't have to worry—they danced off the calories. Someday I might have to watch what I ate and take up heavy-duty exercise, but not now, I thought happily, as I helped myself to a second piece of carrot cake. Carol was the one the weight piled up on, but she didn't seem to worry about being a little plump.

As darkness began to fall, we walked to the football game. The stadium was filling fast, but we had reserved seats with the Pep Club so we didn't have to hurry. Before the game started we mingled with the other red-sweatered girls and discussed our chances of beating Cherry Creek. Fairview High was our biggest rival, but our two high schools were evenly matched. Cherry Creek had won the division title more years than not, so this was our toughest game.

Every Friday night that there was a home game, I was glad we'd joined Pep Club. Our counselor in ninth grade had said, "When you get to high school, join something—anything." It was a good way to mix, to fit into a new school. We did fit in, and I felt it more each week as we got to know more and more girls. Of course, I knew some from my junior high, but you couldn't just stick with the same old people. You needed to get to know juniors and seniors too.

Tonight was our show, marching with the band, being bicycles and runners. The runners were labeled Frank Shorter and Mary Decker and other famous athletes. Carol and I had landed the job of holding the sign that said "finish." We led a cheer every time a runner came over the line.

When we left the field, the crowd roared for us and for the players, who were running back on for the second half. I looked up to see Rob coming right toward me. Quickly I turned and said something to Deb as if I hadn't seen him. Would he notice that I was ignoring him?

Carol went to get us some hot spiced cider, and when it came, steaming and redolent of cinnamon and cloves, I cupped my hands around the mug, absorbing some of the warmth. I was kind of relieved, now that our show was over. I had been so afraid I'd do something dumb like marching off in the wrong direction and make a fool of myself before thousands of screaming fans. Now at least I could relax and enjoy the rest of the game.

I knew Rob's number, of course. He was a receiver. I cringed every time he carried the ball and got tackled. Why didn't I cheer? I still wanted to bang him over the head.

During the rest of the game we yelled and jumped up and down and hugged each other whenever we scored, but for all our encouragement, Hammond lost again. It was close, 21 to

14, but Cherry Creek had this row of two-hundred-pound tackles in their defensive line, and it made the difference.

Why hadn't that loser Harold Tubbs gone out for football instead of band? His extra weight would have counted for something for a change. There he was yelling at us as we started to leave the stadium. Standing there holding a tuba, he looked even more ridiculous than usual, and I wondered if they'd had to get his red uniform specially made.

"Hey, Maggie, want a ride to Pisano's?" Pisano's was a pizza place where everyone went after the games.

"At least it's a ride," Carol whispered. "I was wondering how we'd get there."

Sometimes we just piled in the first car we saw that wasn't full. It would be so great when Carol got her car. Being chauffeured to the pizza parlor by Charles after games really would have been too much, but, on the other hand, you weren't always guaranteed a ride by hitching either.

So we got in the back of Harold's old Chevy. There were other guys in the car too, but we huddled together and ignored them.

"Thanks, Harold," I yelled as he stopped and we jumped out. While we might accept a ride, we certainly didn't want to walk in with them.

I had underestimated Harold's aggressiveness, though. The place was packed with Hammond football fans. There were funny animal faces all over the walls, video games dinged and whirred in the background, and the pepperoni smells were almost unbearably enticing.

"I may die of starvation," I said. "Quick, find a table before they're all gone." We grabbed part of a table and ordered. I had gone to pick up the drinks when the football players started to come in. As Pep Club members we were obligated to lead a cheer for them. I set the three Cokes on our table and stayed in the aisle. Then in my enthusiasm I backed up to the booth behind me.

My yell turned into a shriek. Harold grabbed me from the floor, lifted me up, and literally stuffed me into his booth. There were five guys at a table designed to seat four comfortably— four average-sized people, that is. Now three average-sized people were on one side. Maggie and two more-than-average-sized ones were on the other.

"Harold, let me up!" I was squashed between Harold on the outside and Peter Paul Munzinger on the other side of me. Kids called Peter Paul "Almond Joy." He was a nut, all right, almost as chubby as Harold, and he loved what Harold had pulled on me. How else could he get a girl to sit next to him? He put his arm around me and then offered me a bite of pizza with his free hand.

"No, Peter. I have a pizza coming to my table. Just let me out."

"I saved this slice for you, Maggie. It may just keep you from starving until yours arrives. Now be a good girl and eat." He dangled the delicious-smelling wedge over my mouth, stringing mozarella strands over my nose.

What could I do? Have the cheese and tomato sauce smeared all over my face? I knew these guys. They were persistent with their jokes. I opened my mouth and took a bite. The whole booth cheered. I knew my face was getting as red as tomato sauce, but I stopped fighting and chewed. "Um, delicious, Peter. Did you make it yourself? Does your mother let you cook every night?"

"Only when Harold comes to visit." He held the slice to my mouth again, and strung cheese across the table as he pulled it away. Then Harold held his Coke to my mouth to sip.

"That's a good girl, Maggie. We've noticed how skinny you are. We decided it was our job to fatten you up a bit."

"Harold, don't I hear your mother calling you?" I managed to say before my mouth was full again.

Nothing would do but that I eat the whole slice of pizza, so I relaxed and enjoyed it. Food was food. And sure enough, when I stopped struggling and cooperated, finishing the last bite, Harold stood up and the guys pushed me out of the booth.

I stumbled back to my table, ignoring the catcalls and smart-alec remarks around me. Unfortunately, though, I looked up just in time to see Rob Tyler sitting at a nearby booth filled with junior girls. There was a big smile on his face.

Quickly I sat down and concentrated on our

pizza, which had come while I was being entertained at Harold's table. I grabbed a slice before Debra and Carol ate it all. They were sympathetic, but what good did that do? Once again Rob Tyler had seen me make a fool of myself. I hoped he was glad to see tomato sauce on my face instead of cream foundation.

Before long, the three girls we were sharing our table with got up to leave. "Want a ride home, Debra?" Millie Jessup asked.

"No, thanks," Carol said, before Debra could answer. "We're a long way from being finished. You go on."

"Why'd you do that?" I asked. "How are we going to get home? No way will I ride with Harold again." We hadn't finished eating, but I didn't want to wait till Harold decided it was his duty to see that we got home safely. He lived a block over from me, and he wouldn't know we were staying at Debra's.

"We'll walk if we have to," Carol answered. "Calm down. I'm not ready to go home yet."

She had no more said that when the seats next to us got filled. But not before one chair was picked up and moved. Jamie sat beside Debra. Dobs Cartwright moved the chair and squeezed it in beside Carol. Then I looked up to see Rob Tyler sitting beside me.

Four slizes of pizza did a flip-flop inside my stomach.

# *Chapter 11*

"Get enough to eat?" Rob asked, setting his Coke beside mine.

"For a few minutes," I managed to say, not looking at him. I ran my finger around and around in the little puddle my drink had made. Then my gaze met Debra's. She smiled and rolled her eyes toward Jamie. I shrugged and opened my eyes really wide. It made me feel better to find out she didn't know how to handle this either. Was this what Carol had in mind when she refused a ride home? Did she think this might happen? She certainly had more confidence in miracles happening than I did.

Carol started to chat with the boys about the football game and the plays that Dobs had made, saying that even if they didn't win, it was still a great game. Debra and I took our cue from her and talked football too.

Dobs was the big talker for the guys. I guess it was fitting that he liked Carol, but what would the rest of us do if they decided to go off together?

Rob had some things to say to me, though. Some things I needed to hear.

"You've been ignoring me, Maggie. I guess I don't blame you. You know, I didn't mean to hurt your feelings the other day. I just . . . I mean . . . I wanted you to know I like you the way you are. I guess I didn't say it right. I'm not very experienced at talking to girls. Forgive me?" He took my hand in his.

How could I not forgive him? Some guys wouldn't even notice they'd said the wrong thing. The rest would never apologize. "I guess so," I peeped. I still couldn't look at him but stared down at the red-checkered tablecloth before me, memorizing the pattern. "This time." I squeezed his hand. I can't believe I did that.

Pizza came for the guys, who hadn't ordered till after they sat down with us. Carol used that for her exit line. "You guys must be starving after all that work. And we have to go home." She stood up. I admired her cool. *Go* home. She meant *walk* home, but here she was pretending that she had her car already, not just her learner's permit.

Also she was acting independent instead of sounding desperate for a date. Believe me, I was taking in these lessons as fast as I could compute with my little gray brain cells. The last thing I wanted to do was let go of Rob's hand. But I did.

Before I could stand up, though, Rob took my arm and spoke low in my ear. "You're a good sport, Maggie. I like that in a girl. See you around."

I looked at him then. Blue eyes, big smile. I wanted to say, "Yeah, see you." I couldn't say anything, so I just smiled and left quickly. I had to hope he liked quiet girls too. Why couldn't I say anything? After he thought about it, he'd probably wonder if he wanted to see me again. In a relationship at least one person has to be able to speak.

We started to walk home in the dark.

"How about that!" Carol was ecstatic. "We've got them."

"We do? Where?" I was a bit confused.

"Why didn't you wait and see if they'd give us a ride home, Carol?" Debra asked. "Well, we have to go." Debra mimicked Carol. "Yeah, we have to go walk two miles home."

"It wasn't strategic." Carol skipped along, happy as a clam.

*Strategic?* She'd learned that word at home, I remembered. Did one plan being asked for a date the same way one planned a political campaign? I guess listening and not being seen at dinner has got to have some benefits, after all. Then too, Carol had already had some dates in ninth grade, so she was more experienced.

"What will I do if Rob asks me for a date?" I moaned. "Tell him my mother won't let me go out? I'd rather die."

"We'll figure out something," Carol promised. "Maybe she'll let you double-date or go to parties with a group of kids. She's got to. She can't be that conservative."

Carol was right. I went to parties last year, but Mom or Dad always took me and picked me up. I wouldn't borrow trouble. So far Rob had only said, "See you." He could see me in our two classes or in the halls. And, "Will you study with me sometime?" That could mean in the library. I wished I could believe things could work out. I'd think about it later. Right then I was freezing because of Carol's independence and strategy. We hadn't worn coats to the game, and the night air was starting to get very cold.

Only Debra's promise of cocoa kept me from huddling up in a ball by the side of the road or going back to ask Harold for a ride.

"Isn't this invigorating?" Carol was partly running, partly bouncing along. She was more excited than I'd seen her in a long time.

"Yeah, sure," I agreed. "And I'll probably be out of school with pneumonia for the next three months and Rob will forget I exist."

"He'll bring you flowers and stare at you with his baby blues."

That triggered a fantasy, naturally, and took my mind off my goose bumps for the rest of the way home. Rob said, "You're such a good sport to keep helping me with my algebra while you're dying that I've sent you ten bouquets of red roses." My room would look like a hothouse and all the nurses would hang around to watch my technique with men. They would feel obligated not to let it die with me. It would be called the Howell Technique of Fascinating Men and would be written up in all the books on relationships.

"Learn from her," they'd say. "See how independent she is? She got pneumonia rather than ask for a ride, and now he's coming begging her forgiveness—filled with remorse because he was so unthoughtful."

Finally, numb and exhausted, we stumbled into the trailer. Even in our weakened condition, though, we stayed up half the night giggling and laughing and speculating on dates. Then we slept until noon on Saturday.

Debra had classes all afternoon, so Carol called Charles to come and get us. With her mother gone, Debra had taken two of the children's classes as well as her own.

Carol's excitement over Dobs had not diminished from the night before, and on the way home she thought of a perfect way for us to spend my last night of independence. (My parents were coming back on Sunday, and I'd have to go home.)

I stopped wondering how Gerard was and started to listen when I heard her say "Denver." Denver, what about Denver? "What did you say, Carol? I wasn't listening."

"Stop daydreaming about Rob Tyler and listen to this. How would you like to go see an R-rated movie in Denver—on the big screen at the Cooper? Remember, now's the time to do everything your parents won't let you do when they're home. Otherwise it'll just be a waste."

I didn't really think the last week had been wasted. I had experienced a lot of variety in life-styles and relationships, to begin with, but I tried to stay open to Carol's suggestion.

"How will we get down there?" Somehow I didn't feel quite comfortable breaking in one week *all* the rules I'd lived by for fifteen years. "I've seen a few R-rated movies. My mom always checks to see why they're rated R. Besides, you have to be eighteen to get in, and we don't look that old."

"We'll lie about our age if they ask us. Besides, they don't check as carefully in Denver as they do here. We'll take the bus. I'll tell Mother we have a ride. In fact, I'll tell her we have dates who have a car." I could tell Carol was totally carried away with the idea. I didn't want to be the dud she already thought I was, so I finally said, "Great idea." But my insides rebelled a little. Going to Denver? On the bus? At night? Just the two of us? That felt awfully daring.

Finally I voiced my fears. "Are you sure we have to go to Denver? I'd like to see *Romantically Yours,* and it's playing right here in Cedarhurst."

"Here, they'd never let us in without an adult, you know that. And besides, going to Denver at night will make it a real adventure. *I've* never even done that. And the screen is three times as big as the ones here. Imagine Richard Gere gazing down on you from a triple-sized screen."

I didn't dare say I'd rather look at Rob Tyler in algebra class. I knew that shouldn't seem equally thrilling to me, but there was something about a flesh-and-blood guy who really existed that made the celluloid image of Richard Gere pale in comparison. While I enjoyed my fantasies, I wanted to keep them within the realm of possibility.

"Do you know which buses to take?" If I was going to agree to do this, I needed a plan or a competent leader.

"Sure. Sheri and I planned it out last year,

but then she moved before we could do it. Leave it all to me."

Mrs. Barton was in the kitchen when we got to Carol's place. We had planned that Carol would go up to her room and ask her in private for permission to go. I wondered why Carol didn't just tell Hannah our plan, but maybe there were some things that went over Hannah's head—such as major trips or parties. It was my idea that Carol ask alone because I was pretty sure Mrs. Barton didn't think I was very good company for her daughter. Anyone so low class that she didn't understand burglar alarms wouldn't be considered in Carol's social stratum.

"Carol, dear. What are your plans for the evening? Your Father and I have a dinner engagement. We are being run ragged. Oh, I'll be so glad when this election is over and I can have some time for myself." Mrs. Barton sipped her coffee.

To do what, I wondered. I guessed she and Hubert had been out late Friday night too, run so ragged she'd had to sleep till noon. She was still in her negligée. It was medium blue and all covered with frothy lace.

Oh, I loved that word—*negligée.* "Hand me my negligée, Francine. I won't be getting dressed until noon." It would be peach colored and complement my freckles. Mrs. Barton's complemented her hair. Well, the negligée sure wasn't all ragged and disheveled looking the way her hair was, but the color was good on her. It must have been some party. And all she was having for breakfast—lunch—was, ugh, black coffee.

"We have dates, Mother," Carol lied skillfully. "They're taking us to Denver for dinner and a movie."

"To Denver?" Mrs. Barton raised her eyebrows. Was she going to say no? I crossed my fingers behind my back. While Carol might feel comfortable breaking all *my* rules, I couldn't see her going against her mother's decree.

"Yes. The guys do it all the time. And Dobs has a good car and he's a very safe driver." She was getting warmed up now with her story.

Dobs's car was twenty years old and probably patched together with wire and chewing gum. I tried not to smile and stayed very much in the background.

"Well, I guess that's all right, then. Have a good time." Mrs. Barton stared at the coffee cup that she clutched in both hands. Could she have a hangover? I had never seen anyone with a hangover, but I had read about them, and I had a good imagination. You would probably not want to argue with anyone about anything, and even talking or listening very much would be painful.

We ran upstairs before she could wake up any more and have second thoughts. "See how easy that was?" Carol clapped her hands. "Now we'll dress up, of course. You can wear my green outfit again and borrow some makeup."

"Just a little," I said quickly. "I have to get used to that look a little at a time."

To my dismay I couldn't help feeling that I did need to get used to all this freedom a little bit at a time. The evening's upcoming adventure made me feel as if I'd gone overboard. And did I mention, I'm not a good swimmer either? Especially in an ocean as vast as Denver.

# *Chapter 12*

Since we wanted to go to the seven o'clock movie, we had to leave Cedarhurst at three-thirty. It would take an hour on the bus to get to downtown Denver, then another hour to transfer and get to south Denver where the theater with the wide screen was located and Richard Gere was playing.

We sneaked out of Carol's house because we couldn't very well ask Charles to drive us after we'd said our dates had cars.

"Where are we going to eat dinner?" I asked when we'd successfully completed step one. We'd gotten from Carol's bus stop to Cedarhurst, bought tickets for Denver, and were sitting side by side with the Saturday commuters. The RTD bus whooshed away from the station on Walnut Street, and we were off on our adventure—for better or worse. I fought the urge to cross my legs since crossing my fingers would be too obvious, and I was trying to act as enthusiastic and calm as Carol.

"Oh, Maggie. Try to think about something except your stomach for a change. We'll get hot dogs at the theater and then popcorn or whatever you need. I've got lots of money."

I didn't have much left after our shopping

and eating sprees, but I'd paid for my bus ticket and had money for the movie. I found I didn't like Carol making me feel self-conscious about my eating habits, though. A friend should never make you feel bad about anything, especially something you couldn't help. Did I try to make her feel self-conscious about being rich? No. She couldn't help that either.

What was that saying about how you can never be too rich or too thin? Thank goodness I have one of those attributes, but I'll be glad when people stop saying *skinny* and say *willowy* or *slim*. And Carol should just accept by now that I have to eat a lot instead of making me feel guilty when I'm hungry.

The bus made several stops before it left town, and we looked everyone over who got on going to Denver. There were only a few young people, and they were in their twenties. One couple put skis underneath where the baggage rode. They must be catching the train to Winter Park. Then the bus sped onto the turnpike, and there was no turning back. Several fields zipped by, then the subdivisions that formed the bedroom communities of Broomfield and Westminster filled the window scene.

"Relax, Maggie. Aren't you having fun?" Carol asked. "I'll bet you've never done anything even close to this exciting."

I was sure I must have, but I didn't search my memory. "Sure I'm having fun, Carol. But how did you know I was nervous?"

"You always get quiet when you're nervous.

You didn't say two words to Rob Tyler last night."

"I didn't know what to say." I had never told Debra or Carol about what Rob had said to me last night. Having a guy say you're a good sport is a nice compliment, but it isn't in the same category as his saying you're beautiful or sexy. I figured they'd just laugh. But then they didn't have to deal with Harold's antics. He only picked on me. Did that mean he only liked me? Lucky Maggie. Wouldn't it be funny if Harold had helped me get Rob's attention? The pool dunking, the pizza caper. Rob was falling in love with me because of Harold's tricks? There was some kind of justice in that.

Carol started giving me a lecture on how to talk to guys. I decided I'd better listen. It passed the time till we pulled into the downtown bus station.

There were a couple of movie theaters right in the heart of Denver, but they'd gotten kind of seedy and weren't where we wanted to go. Denver itself was always exciting to me. I gawked at the skyscrapers as if I'd just come in from Kansas. We have a height limit in Cedarhurst, so our tallest buildings are only five or six stories and there are only a couple of those.

We skipped along the brick mall, once avoiding a man asleep on the sidewalk and another time a woman with a shopping cart full of bottles and cans. Most shoppers had gone home.

Window-shopping would have been fun too since there are tons of great clothing stores on the new Sixteenth Street Mall. But we had to hurry to find the corner where a bus going east to Colorado Boulevard and then south stopped. Carol had studied the bus schedule and a street map, so she proved to be a good tour guide. We made the connection with minutes to spare.

I started to feel better. It wasn't as though we were in some foreign country. Everyone spoke English. The buses were well marked. This wasn't such a big deal. There was no way we could miss the theater. It was a huge, round building.

There was already a line for the seven o'clock showing, so I was glad we hadn't cut it too close. How awful it would have been to get here and have the movie sold out. And Carol was right. We had no trouble getting in in the midst of such a big crowd. We got seats and then took turns going out for food. Carol went first, then came back and handed me a five-dollar bill. She knew I had about finished off my vacation allowance.

I had stopped feeling guilty about her treating me a long time ago. There was no way I could keep up with her spending habits, and I hoped that having her eat at my house lots of times balanced it out.

The hot dogs smelled even better than the popcorn, and I got a big drink to wash down the two I bought. I got the popcorn too, though, for later when the hot dogs were gone. Then, for good measure, I added a box of Dots in case I got hungry halfway through the film and couldn't bear to leave for even a minute.

I was glad I was well fortified. The movie was super. Lots of kissing, some violence, of course, since it was a gangster movie. But not a lot of gore, which I hated. I hadn't minded missing the *Halloween* series of movies at all. And I knew Mom was right when she said those types of movies make victims of women. They also made all women seem helpless and dumb. I scrunched down in my seat when there was more nudity than I'd ever seen before. How embarrassed I'd have been if I was with Rob. I was glad we didn't have dates.

"Wow, that was awesome, wasn't it?" Carol started talking as we left the theater. She has trouble being quiet for two hours, but someone behind us said "hush" the second time she whispered to me, so she had saved her comments until the movie was over.

"Yeah, it was fine." I thought about how tickled my mother would be because parts of it had made me feel uncomfortable.

"I love Richard Gere. I think Dobs looks a lot like him, don't you?" Carol pulled on her jacket. We'd been smarter about dressing warmly tonight, remembering it was October.

Frankly, I didn't see much resemblance between Dobs Cartwright and Richard Gere, but then Richard Gere had a tiny mustache in this movie and his hair was all slicked down in a funny style. "Sure," I said, willing to agree anyway since it didn't matter that much to me.

"Hey, let's get some ice cream. You must be hungry again by now, Maggie." Carol pointed to a Swensen's across the street in the shopping center near the theater.

I hated to admit it, but I was, so I was glad it

was Carol's suggestion. It had gotten dark, reminding me we were a long way from home, but it was only nine o'clock. The Swensen's was brightly lit, which made me feel better. And then I felt positively wonderful when we looked at the menu. We ordered sundaes, and when they came, piled with whipped cream and butterscotch, we dug in.

Carol chattered away about the movie while I savored every bite of our gooey treat. So when she stopped talking, I looked up. Her mouth was frozen open, and she held her spoon, dripping, in midair. Had Richard Gere, or Dobs Cartwright—or both—just entered the ice cream parlor?

She lowered her voice. "We may have a problem, Maggie. Sit tight and let me do the talking.

I had no intention of going anywhere. Trouble? What kind of trouble? Did I dare look around? Then I didn't have to. A hand slapped our table. On the hand were three rings. One was black and had a skull mounted on the black stone. The forearm was hairy right down to the wrist, which was encircled with a leather bracelet. The leather was dotted with silver studs.

The farther upward my eye traveled, the worse the situation looked. Four guys stood by our booth. They were all dressed like heavy-metal punkers—black leather pants and vests, except that the guy that rested his paw on our table had on a sleeveless leopard-skin top. All of them wore lots of chains and silver decorations on the black leather. Their arms were bare, despite the cool evening, and tattooed with hearts and flowers and daggers, things like that. Maybe they'd hung their leather jackets up neatly when they came in.

Three of them had shoulder-length hair, black too. But one had braids, so blond they were almost white. He had black eye shadow all around his eyes, and he smiled at me till a shiver ran down my back. Then he put his hand on my shoulder. I shrugged it off, and he smiled again.

We have some punkers in Cedarhurst, but since we've known most of them since third grade, we just label them weird and figure it's a stage they're going through. No one in Cedarhurst looked like these guys, though. Maybe they'd just come from playing a concert downtown and had stopped for ice cream on the way home.

They looked older than high school. They had to be in their twenties, at least. Casually, I hoped, I focused on the table in front of me and shoveled in another bite of butterscotch; but somehow I couldn't swallow. Icy syrup trickled over my back tooth that's sensitive to cold.

"Lookee here, guys," the leader of the motor heads said. "These two chickees are out past their bedtime."

I didn't even mind his recognizing we weren't as old as we'd tried to look. Maybe they didn't like children. Maybe I should just tell them right away that we were only fifteen and that our mothers were coming to pick us up any minute.

He pushed me over and sat beside me. One of the other guys sat next to Carol. I was really scared now. How could we get out? The guy beside me smelled all sweaty, and there was liquor on his breath. They had definitely not started their evening with ice cream.

"Go away, stupid," Carol said, "or I'll call the manager." Why didn't she just keep quiet? I'd never have said anything. I would have totally ignored them. But *could* we ignore them?

"Go ahead. She's Lenny's woman." The hulk pointed to a tall, skinny girl whose hair was snow white. She grinned at us. That figured. We were in their territory, even in the ice cream parlor. I wondered why there weren't more customers after the movie. Did everyone around here know the place was terrorized by followers of Conan the Barbarian?

"Leave the babies alone till closing time, Lenny," Blond Braids said. "That one you're sitting by is mine, anyway. I saw her first, and you've got Berta."

Carol had gotten the message to keep quiet; her threats were empty anyway if these guys were connected with the management. We just kept eating, although I was really feeling sick. Maybe I could throw up on their dry-clean-only outfits.

Why hadn't I had the nerve to suggest to Carol, or even insist, that it wasn't safe for us to go to Denver alone? Especially when we'd have to return after dark. I didn't really know who these creeps were, but I knew they weren't just weird like some of the characters in Cedarhurst. These guys were half drunk and looking for trouble.

Were they on motorcycles or in a car? If they

tried to force Carol and me to get into a car with them, there wouldn't be much we could do. Most of them were twice our size.

Finally they slithered into the booth across from us, but they kept on grinning. Were they waiting for us to leave? How long could you make a sundae called Top of the Iceberg last? We should have ordered Volcanoes, which erupted with chocolate lava flowing down from a height of twelve inches. If you could get through two, you got the second one free.

A black-haired waitress, hair frizzed about two feet out from her head, came over to tell us it was closing time. I looked at my watch. It was only ten o'clock, but on the other hand, we'd been there almost an hour. "Anything else? We're getting ready to close."

I was about to say "A police escort to the bus stop, please," when I noticed her ring. Matching skulls. How cute. She was probably not the hulk's twisted sister either.

"No, thank you. Do you have a phone?" I asked, pushing aside my half-finished dessert and acting as if I always paid two dollars for ice cream and then didn't eat it.

"Yeah, there's one outside on the corner by the drugstore."

"Oh, thank you. My father said he'd pick us up when we phoned. He lives only five minutes away from here. We've been to the movie. Have you seen it? You'd really like it." I chattered on and on, trying to sound casual.

I got up, hoping she'd relay my message to her friends. Surely she wouldn't want her mate chasing after us anyway. But then maybe the other two guys were without girls, and sister liked even numbers. We'd do in a pinch even if our clothes were all wrong.

We grabbed our coats and left while she was still there. I led the way quickly to the front door. Carol threw a five-dollar bill from her shoulder bag at the cashier, telling her to give the waitress a tip for us. Maybe she could use it to give the tattoo I knew was under her sleeve a touch-up.

"Think they'll follow us?" Carol whispered, her bravado gone.

"They might be looking for entertainment while the girlfriends clean up." I jerked my arms into the sleeves of my coat and pulled it tightly around me.

"Let's run to the next bus stop. It's probably only a couple of blocks north," Carol suggested.

I looked in that direction. As soon as the small shopping center ended, it was pitch black. "No, let's go this way." I pointed south. "It's lighter, and you can't see out of the ice cream parlor in this direction. They'll think we got our ride." Boy, would I have been glad to see my dad in his car right then, no matter what the consequences.

Carol had on high heels. I was glad then that we didn't wear the same size shoes. I'd had to wear my school flats, as usual.

"Come on, hurry," I puffed, my shoulder bag banging against me with every step. I grabbed it and held it still.

"I can't run any faster." Carol gasped for

breath, and she started to limp. "Look and see if they're coming."

I didn't really want to know if they were. But while I waited for her to catch up, I looked back down the sidewalk toward the parking lot of the shopping center.

We hadn't gotten far enough away for the coast to be clear. Blond Braids and his buddy had come outside the ice cream parlor and were looking in our direction. He pointed toward us and then they both turned and headed for an old Camaro that was parked near the front of Swensen's.

"Carol!" I clutched her arm. "They're going to follow us. What'll we do?"

# Chapter 13

"We can't get away." I grabbed Carol's arm and tugged her along with me. "They have a car. They'll just cruise the block a couple of times until they spot us, no matter how far we run."

"Look, there's the bus," Carol gasped.

Nothing had ever looked so good, and if we hadn't run, we'd have missed it. We'd have had to wait on the street corner for another half hour. Talk about luck. Thank you, guardian angel.

We clattered up the metal steps, then searched our purses for correct change. I had visions of the driver putting us off right at the next bus stop in front of Swensen's when we had all we needed but a quarter. "Sorry," he'd say, "but you have to have correct change."

Again luck was with us. Our six quarters clanged in the box, and quickly we pushed through the crowd and ran toward the back of the bus. We flopped down and pretended to be tying our shoes. Anyone watching would have thought we were crazy since Carol's shoes had bows and mine were flat-heeled pumps. I started to giggle then, whether out of relief or fear or stupidity, I can't explain.

Knowing again that anyone observing would

think us silly teenage girls, we kept our heads down for a couple of blocks. There had to be some advantages to all grown-ups thinking fifteen-year-olds were either demented or well on their way to being so.

When I finally peeked out and whispered, "All clear," we sat up. Carol put her head on my shoulder and hugged me close. I knew she'd been scared too.

"Oh, Maggie, you really kept your cool. I was so scared," she admitted.

It wasn't the first time I'd used my parents' strict rules to get me out of something I really didn't want to do anyway, so the story about my father picking me up had come to me naturally.

"Oh, it was nothing," I said modestly. I knew then that I was destined to become one of the finest actresses Hammond High had ever seen. Everyone in the cast could forget their lines, and I'd cover for them. She's cool under pressure, people would say. She saved the whole play.

We rode in silence for a few blocks. The bus emptied fast, and soon there was hardly anyone left, so the bus driver skipped most stops and zoomed right along. I kept looking for a Camaro to pull up beside us or behind us, but I guess the hoods gave up easily.

"I guess I'm glad we don't live in Denver," Carol said finally.

"Yeah. Cedarhurst feels a lot safer. The only heavy metal we have is Harold's tuba." Suddenly I had this vision of Harold in black leather and studs and nearly started laughing hysterically.

Carol giggled. "Or if we lived in Denver, maybe we'd know the places to go and the places to stay out of."

"Or maybe we'd have known wicked sister since kindergarten and remembered that once she was only plain Suzy Guggisberg."

"And that then her hair was dishwater blond, her shoes leather, and her bracelets plastic bangles from K-Mart."

We kept saying silly things to cover our real feelings. Then we got quiet again. I guess both of us would hate to admit it, but we were tired. The narrow escape had just about finished us off.

Suddenly Carol said, "Maggie, do you notice anything funny?"

I thought we were still acting silly. I looked at my fingers, my toes, then got a mirror from my purse. "No more than usual."

"Stop clowning. It's all dark outside."

"Yes. In case you hadn't noticed, it got dark while we were in the movie. It's night now. Ten-thirty, if you want to know exactly."

"Maggie, we're in neighborhoods with houses. We should be downtown by now. Office buildings. Skyscrapers. We're on the wrong bus!"

I looked out. Carol was right. There were only houses and an occasional streetlight. "What'll we do?"

"Get off." Carol pulled the cord to signal we wanted the next stop. "We'll get a bus going back in the direction we've come, and we'll ask the driver where to transfer."

As soon as the bus stopped, we jumped out

the back door. But somehow when it whooshed away, leaving us in a cloud of acrid fumes, I felt abandoned.

"Maybe we should have asked *this* driver the best way to get downtown." I felt a terrible need to ask someone, anyone, what to do next. I had used up most of my resources dealing with the hulks. And my faith in Carol's knowledge of Denver, bus schedules, maps, adventures was fading fast.

"We can just cross the street and look for a bus going in the other direction," Carol said again, like a recording. "Don't panic now, Maggie. I'll get us home."

I followed Carol across the street, all too empty of traffic at this hour of the night. We walked toward the lights we could see on the corner, though, since where we were standing was dark. By the time we found the next red sign that signaled a bus stop, we were in a small shopping area: a bookstore, a drugstore, a deli—all closed, of course. But more traffic ran north and south. At least Carol said it was north and south.

I looked at the street sign. "It's University. We're way over by the University of Denver, Carol."

"Then we aren't lost. If we know where we are, we aren't lost. Right?"

Why did I get the idea that Carol needed some assurance that we weren't lost? "Right," I said, with as much confidence as I could muster. "What time do the buses stop running?" I had to add.

"They run all night." Carol studied her map.

"See." She spread it out for me. "Here's University. We can go straight back west and get back to Colorado Boulevard, and then we take the bus north like we should have a while ago."

I didn't want to remind Carol that we'd end up right back at Swensen's, but surely the two of us weren't exciting enough for the motorheads to hang around and wait for. They'd have taken their women home long ago.

While we waited for the bus, I imagined this pad with black leather bean-bag chairs and skull-shaped lights hanging from the ceiling by silver chains.

Carol's yelling interrupted my creating a proper atmosphere for hard-rock rebels. "Maggie! My purse! Where's my purse?"

Carol had on a P-coat, except that it had epaulets on the shoulders. She always buttoned one epaulet over the strap of her purse so it wouldn't slip off. I looked closer. Some of the strap was still there. I pulled it out, and for a second both of us stared at the tiny leather thong that had once been attached to a small leather purse. The edges were clearly cut, and it was easy to figure out what had happened.

Carol had sat on the outside of the double bus seat. While we'd had our heads down, distracted by our fear of being followed, someone in the crowd had carefully, cleanly stolen her purse.

"You had all the money." Even though I knew it wasn't her fault, my voice accused her of being careless. I needed someone to blame for our predicament. "I put my last quarter in for my fare out here."

"What'll we do?" Carol's voice quavered, and I knew it was up to me to remain cool again.

"Okay," I said with confidence, the experienced actress taking over. "We've got only one choice. We find a phone, call your mother collect, and have someone come after us."

"No, Maggie. I can't do that! Don't even ask me to do that. My parents would kill me." Carol started to cry. Not tears or little whimpering noises, but big, hysterical sobs. She was obviously more afraid of her parents than she was of the mess we were in.

"Well, I guess we could stay here till morning, get jobs until we've earned five dollars or so, and then . . ." I couldn't get Carol's attention with my new idea. I held her in my arms in dismay. I'd never seen her break down like this. In fact, she always seemed so much in charge of her life and herself.

My mother would kill me too, and I might be grounded for the rest of the school year, but she *would* come and get me—us. And I *would* call her if I could. But *my* parents weren't home. It wouldn't do me a lot of good to call collect to Chicago and say, "Here I am, your errant daughter, stranded in Denver. Come get me." I wondered how long it took to wire money. I'd seen those television commercials where someone in trouble called home and said, "Send money. Fast."

Okay, Miss Actress, Star-to-Be. Saver of Performances on Stage with Your Cool. Save this situation. Obviously it was up to me. Carol was blubbering even harder now. What would Jane Fonda do? What would Meryl Streep do? I guess they'd shoot the scene again, get it right this time. But I didn't know any stage actresses to call on. The only stage play I'd ever seen was our junior high's version of *The Wizard of Oz*, and I didn't have on red shoes, nor was there a tin man or a scarecrow in sight.

However, before I could make any intelligent decisions, the nightmare we thought was over picked up right where it had left off. A black Camaro with orange and yellow flames consuming the doors and crackling toward the swooped-up tail cruised to a stop across the street from us. There was no time and no place to hide. The doors swung open, and a whole regiment of heavy metal set black leather boots on the pavement.

Blond Braids looked at me and grinned.

# *Chapter 14*

"Maggie!" Carol had stopped blubbering, but now she started up again with little whimpers like a kicked dog.

There was time for my brain to signal only one command. Run! I grabbed Carol's arm and tugged her around the corner. Where we'd go was anyone's guess. *Away* was the first destination. *Home* I wished.

Only one place in the block ahead showed any signs of life. A sign outside said THE PUB. It was a bar. Could we get into any more trouble by going inside? I never hesitated. There was no choice.

The interior was so dimly lit I could barely see, but the clink of glasses and low conversational tones reassured me there were people inside. A plan took shape. I clutched Carol's sweaty hand and headed for the ladies' room I figured would be in the back.

Then suddenly the limp body I was pulling along behind me became rigid, anchored to the floor, and slammed me to a stop.

"Carol, come on. I have a plan." Then I looked to see why she had stopped.

"Carol?" a familiar voice said. "And Maggie? Whatever are you doing here?"

It was Perkins. I mean Charles, Carol's parents' chauffeur, looking a lot younger and a lot cuter than he did in his uniform. Or had I never looked at him that well? He had been like a part of the car. What was he doing in this bad dream? Was I totally hallucinating? I imagined it was reasonable that I would dream up someone safe from my past. My father . . . Gerard . . . turned into a guard dog. But Charles?

I will never again question my nimble responses under fire, however. I didn't spend any more time wondering why Charles was here in our nightmare. "Please," I urged him and his companion, a very pretty girl. "Let us sit on the inside. Hurry."

As if this had all been planned, the two of them stood up, not even asking for the script, and let us slide into the old wooden booth. Then they sat back down. I did see an exchange of puzzled looks, but obviously they were intrigued by this unexpected interruption of their evening.

I guess our actions were explained by the clank and swagger of the three guys bursting through the door, looking totally out of place in the college bar.

"Friends of yours?" Charles questioned me. Carol had her head down on the table.

"Acquaintances," I acknowledged, looking straight at Charles and not anyplace else. Surely they'd concede that we'd won.

"Would it be correct to assume you'd like a ride home?" Charles asked, finishing his beer.

Carol came to life. "Oh, Charles, could you?

We'd be forever indebted to you. And will you absolutely swear afterward that you never saw us tonight?" Carol used her desperate, this-is-a-matter-of-life-or-death voice.

Charles looked at me.

"It's a long story," I said. "Tell you on the way home."

In silent agreement the four of us waited a few minutes before we stood up and left the pub. Outside I breathed a sigh of relief. There was no sign of our admirers. We had escaped being gun molls or heavy-metal molls—whatever—and it was an experience I was glad to forgo.

Charles's friend had her own car in the parking lot, so maybe he hadn't planned on taking her home. I hated to think we'd broken up a good date for him. I said so when we got in his battered old Chevy.

"It's okay, Maggie. I just met her tonight."

"She may think twice about seeing you again after this."

"Oh, I think she may be curious enough to want to hear the rest of the story." He smiled, and I knew he wanted to know too but was too polite to ask.

I volunteered the highlights of our evening, figuring he had a right to know. Carol sat quietly in the backseat. I had gotten in the front, not wanting Charles—or Chuck, as his new friend had called him—to feel like a chauffeur on what must have been his night off.

"Lucky I was down here, wasn't it?"

It went way beyond being lucky. "What *are*

you doing here?" I suppose it wasn't any of my business, but I'd shared our evening. And I was curious about his.

"I'm taking a class at the university. Novel Writing. Promise you won't laugh, and I'll confess that I'm writing a mystery novel."

Our Charles, a novelist? "I think that's wonderful, Charles. But why aren't you taking it in Cedarhurst so you don't have to drive way down here?"

"I took a class at Cedarhurst Community last year, but I need more help. The teacher here writes mystery novels."

"I guess you could put in a chapter about the narrow escape of your detective after a run-in with a heavy-metal gang."

Charles laughed. "You never know when that scene might come in handy. A novelist uses everything that happens to him in his stories."

We got quiet. Maybe I could use the night's adventure—now that we'd escaped safely—in my own novel. When it made the best-seller list, I'd use the money I made to go and relax on the Riviera. "Oh, look," people would say, "that's the famous writer Magnolia Howell. You know, she wrote that funny novel about the punk-rock gang that terrorized Denver until they were tumbled from power by two young teenagers."

I was looking over my royalty statements, deciding if I had enough money to go to Paris too, when we pulled in the drive at Carol's. Charles lived in the apartment over the garage, an artist's garret, I imagined, so he stopped there.

"Thank you, Charles," Carol said quietly.

"Anytime. Glad to be of service, ma'am." Charles looked at me and grinned. Somehow I felt we probably had some thoughts and opinions in common. I vowed to talk to him more when we rode with him again.

Moving out of the garage light and into the shadows of the yard, I followed Carol to the house. Quietly she opened the door with her key and ran to punch in the computer code so the burglar alarm wouldn't go off.

We tiptoed through the hall, Carol now carrying her shoes. Her panty hose were in shreds. In the living room Mrs. Barton lay half on, half off of a couch, fast asleep and snoring softly. She was still in an evening dress, her hair mussed, makeup smeared. Had she tried to be the motherly type and wait up for us? Or had she passed out before she could get upstairs?

I had this impulse to shake her awake long enough to tell her we were home. For my own peace of mind, if not hers. But Carol put her finger over her lips, and we sneaked on up the stairs.

We were too tired to talk, and a bed never looked so good. I didn't even have time to go back over in my mind the sixteen narrow escapes we'd had getting home. To Carol's house, I corrected my thinking, and fell asleep.

Next thing I knew, Carol's phone was ringing, and it was broad daylight. It was on my side of the bed, so I picked up the receiver before Carol fully woke up.

"Maggie. It's Mother. We're home. A taxi just

dropped us off, but I couldn't wait to talk to you. How are you?"

"Fine," I managed to say, pulling myself to a sitting position and trying to wake up. "I'm fine now."

"Now? What do you mean *now*? Weren't you fine yesterday, this week?" Mother sounded concerned.

"Oh, sure. I just said that. I've been fine all week." I shook myself to get wide-awake. One more slip was all Mom would need to start worrying or probing for some answers and information.

"I've missed you. We're coming right out to get you. Can you be ready in half an hour?"

I realized that I had been ready three days ago. "Sure, Mom. I'll be ready."

I slipped out of bed. Carol had mumbled something when the phone rang, then turned over and went back to sleep. Quickly I got dressed and packed my suitcase. I didn't worry about forgetting anything, though. Carol could bring it to me the next time she stayed at my house.

I got downstairs without seeing anyone except Felicity the cat. "Good-bye, Felicity," I whispered. "Thank you for an interesting week." And informative, I added as I hesitated at the front door. How could I get out without knowing the code? Was I trapped in the Barton mansion forever?

No. I hurried to the kitchen and the back door. To my relief, Hannah sat dozing in the sun coming in through the back screen. The door was wide open. Earphones on, she had her Walkman tucked into the crook of her arm. I unlatched the storm door and escaped.

Now why did I use that word?

Mom was walking toward the front door. I ran to meet her, and she hugged me tightly. I hugged back. Daddy got out to put my suitcase in the trunk, and I hugged him first. He smelled of shaving lotion, and his cheek was smooth.

"Did you tell Mrs. Barton you had a nice time?" Mom asked after we got into the car. "And I want you to write her a nice letter."

"I think she was still asleep." I ran my hands over the vinyl of the backseats and fingered the hole that Gerard's toenails had torn the last time he went to the vet.

"Still asleep? It's eleven o'clock." Mother was aghast.

"Well, she was . . . out last night."

"Oh. I guess they do have a busy social life."

"Yes, they do. Very busy."

"Are you going to be able to do without a butler, and a maid, and a cook, Maggie?" Dad teased as he pushed the hair out of his eyes.

I realized I'd missed seeing him do that. "I guess I can stand it. How's Gerard?"

Mother started telling me how glad Gerard was to see them and about their trip, but I hardly listened. I was thinking about Carol and about me. My life. How I was going to invite Carol over next weekend to spend the night. I'd give her a big hug. I'd maneuver her into Mom's path so Mom would hug her too. She probably still wasn't ready for a hug from Dad, but that was okay.

We'd mess up the kitchen making popcorn balls. Dad would tell me to shut the refrigerator door when I'd stand there finding us something to drink. Mom would ask us if we couldn't find anything more stimulating to watch on TV than "Destinies."

In other words, nothing would have really changed. Except me. I think I just took one of those giant steps toward getting older. I might backslide next week when Dad gives me my allowance, reluctantly. But I'd hang around with him and Mom till I got it right. Growing up.

"You hungry, Maggie?" Dad asked. "Did they feed you enough over there?" We'd gotten home and Dad stood looking in the refrigerator.

"Not today." I went over and stood beside him. "You're wasting electricity standing there. Did you buy stock in the company while you were in Chicago?"

"Not hardly, and you're right. Besides, there's nothing here. Want to go to the grocery store with me?" Dad put his arm round me and squeezed hard.

"Sure, Dad."

"Hey, wait for me." Mom put her shoes on. "I'll tag along."

Gerard hurried up to us. I looked at Dad, who nodded.

"Okay, Gerard, you good-for-nothing hound. You can go too. Just this once. And then I have a friend who'd like to visit you."

Gerard jumped on me and knocked me onto the couch.

"Maggie, do be careful. I hope you didn't act that way at the Bartons. They probably have really nice furniture. It's a good thing we don't have really expensive stuff here."

Yeah, Mom, I said to myself. It's a good thing. It's a really good thing.

We were all hungry, so we bought out half the grocery store. Dad groaned when the total came up on the register, but he winked at me and paid.

"I thought teenage girls dieted full-time."

"She got your metabolism, Dave," Mom said. "So you can't complain." Mom moved up beside him and put her arm around his waist.

"She got your cute little rear." Dad patted Mom and her face turned red.

"Dave. We're in public." She grabbed a bag of groceries and hurried to escape from the store.

I should have been as embarrassed as Mom, but somehow I wasn't. For once I didn't care who saw my parents acting like newlyweds in public. Not that I'd ever act that way, but—

"Here, Maggie." Dad handed me two bags. "You can at least help carry all this."

Back in the kitchen Mom put stuff away while Dad started browning meat for spaghetti and I put a pan of water on the stove to boil.

"Want garlic bread?" Mom asked. "I can take a loaf from the freezer."

"Do I?" My mouth watered. I'd had my fill of tiny French rolls. Mom made her own white bread and put garlic and butter on it when we had spaghetti or lasagna. It seemed like years since I'd had spaghetti.

"I'd forgotten how cute you are, Maggie." Dad bumped my ponytail so it swung to and fro. "Were you this cute when we left?"

I looked down at my sweats, which Gerard had muddied on the way home, realizing that tonight I didn't have to dress for dinner.

"Probably. If you like freckles," I answered. "Want to play Trivial Pursuit after we eat?"

"Sure. Unless you've been practicing for a week."

I'd been practicing, all right, practicing being a lady, practicing being rich, practicing being sophisticated and beautiful. Fortunately, I decided, I hadn't gotten good at any of those things.

But I had gotten better at being me. If I got a question that said, What fifteen-year-old Cedarhurst girl voluntarily went back to her parents' home to serve out her term of parental supervision, I'd know what my answer would be.

Magnolia Howell. The remaining years were difficult, but she survived.

"I'm going to win tonight, Dad, so don't get your hopes up." I put my arm around him and watched him stir the hamburger. Mom laughed and moved to hug me from the other side. Gerard barked, wanting his share of the loving.

Fortunately there was enough to go around.